William Henry Withrow

The King's Messenger

Lawrence Temple's Probation

William Henry Withrow

The King's Messenger
Lawrence Temple's Probation

ISBN/EAN: 9783743403444

Manufactured in Europe, USA, Canada, Australia, Japa

Cover: Foto ©Andreas Hilbeck / pixelio.de

Manufactured and distributed by brebook publishing software (www.brebook.com)

William Henry Withrow

The King's Messenger

PREFACE.

THE following Story is an attempt to depict, from personal observation, phases of Canadian life with which the writer is somewhat familiar—with what success others must decide. If it shall inspire in our readers a stronger love of that noble country, and a desire to live for its moral and religious progress, it will not have been written in vain. It is especially hoped that the religious lessons which it is designed to teach may lead its readers to a fuller consecration of all their powers and faculties to the glory of God and the welfare of their fellow-men.

W. H. W.

RIVER LANDING ON THE OTTAWA.

CONTENTS.

CHAPTER VII.

CHAPTER VIII.

CHAPTER IX.

CHAPTER X.

CHAPTER XI.

CHAPTER XII.

CHAPTER XIII.

CHAPTER XIV.

CHAPTER XV.

CHAPTER XVI.

" A GENTLE knight was pricking on the plaine,
.   .   .   .
And on his brest a bloodie crosse he bore,
The deare remembrance of his dying Lord,
For Whose sweete sake that glorious badge he wore,
And dead, as living, ever Him ador'd :
Upon his shield the like was also scor'd,
For soveraine hope, which in His helpe he had.
Right, faithful, true he was in deed and word ;
But of his cheere did seeme too solemne sad ;
Yet nothing did he dread, but ever was ydrad."

SPENSER—*Faerie Queene.*

THE KING'S MESSENGER;

OR,

LAWRENCE TEMPLE'S PROBATION.*

A STORY OF CANADIAN LIFE

CHAPTER I.

TWO PARTINGS.

"The parting word must still be spoken,
Though the anguished heart be broken ,
But in yonder bright forever
Pain and parting can come never."

"MY son, how can I give you up?"
"You will have brother Tom and the girls,
mother ; and you know it is better that I should go."

* The writer of this story, illustrative of Canadian life and
character, deems it right to say that, with scarce an exception,
every incident therein recorded has come under his own experience or observation, or has been certified by credible testimony.
In the dialect conversations almost every word and phrase have
been repeatedly noted by himself as occurring in Canadian communities.   For obvious reasons persons and places are presented
under pseudonyms which in some cases will reveal as much as
they conceal.

1

"Yes, my boy; but that does not make it any easier to lose you. You seemed almost to fill your father's place. You grow more like him every day."

"Well, that is not much of a compliment to his beauty, mother dear."

"Handsome is that handsome does, my boy. I am sure that God's smile and your father's blessing will follow you wherever you go, for no son was ever kinder to his mother."

"I should be unworthy of the name I bear if I did not do all I could for the best mother in the world. But Tom is now old enough to look after the out-of-door work, and Mary, the trustees have promised me, shall have my school, and Nellie will help you in the house. I shall earn lots of money, mother, and be able to spare some for you and save enough for a few terms at college."

"It was your father's dying wish, my boy, and though it is like tearing out a piece of my heart to have you go, yet I will not oppose it. We shall get along nicely, I trust, without your help, although we shall miss you very much ; but I fear you will suffer in those dreadful woods, and so far away too. It was your father's prayer for years, my son, that you might become 'THE KING'S MESSENGER,' as he used to call it, and I am sure I have no loftier ambition than to see you a faithful preacher as your father was."

"If God should call me, mother, to that holy work, I am sure He will open a way for me. But now my duty clearly is to earn all I can and learn all I can."

"God bless you, my boy ; " and the voice trembled a little as it spoke. "You were my first-born, and you are the child of many prayers. The fondest hopes of a father passed into the skies were centred upon you. I feel sure that you will not disappoint them."

"Amen!" was the response, deeply and solemnly uttered as if it were a dedication, and after a pause the speaker continued, "Mother, I want you to give me father's Bible, the one he kept upon his study table. As I read the notes and references in his own writing, it seems as though he were speaking to me from the silent page."

" You shall have it, my boy ; and may it be as a spell to keep you in the hour of temptation and trial."

" It will, mother, I am sure. I have only to read my father's Bible, and to think of my father's prayers, to be strengthened to endure any trial and to withstand any temptation."

Conversing in such a strain this mother and son sat long in the quiet dusk that gradually filled the little room. The after-glow of the sunset gleamed softly in the west, and as they sat side by side in the fading light they strikingly recalled the beautiful picture by Ary Scheffer of Monica and Augustine, that holy mother and heroic son whose memory has come down to us through fifteen centuries. On the face of this Canadian mother, though thin and wan and worn with care and marked with sorrow, was a look of unutterable peace. The deep calm brown eyes, which were not unused to tears, looked into the glowing west as though the heavens opened to her gaze. A rapt expression beamed upon her countenance as though she held communion with the loved and lost, whose feet, which had kept time with hers in the march of life, now walked the golden streets of the New Jerusalem. At such an hour as this

> " O very near seem the pearly gates,
> And sweetly the harpings fall,
> And the soul is restless to soar away,
> And longs for the angel's call."

The pure white brow seemed the home of holy thoughts, and the soft hair, streaked with silver threads, was brushed smoothly back beneath the pathetic widow's cap. The face of the boy was lighted up with an eager enthusiasm. The firm-set mouth indicated indomitable energy. The fire of youth sparkled in his eye, but a peculiar manly tenderness softened his countenance as he looked upon his mother. For a time they sat together in silence; then, withdrawing her gaze from the sky, in which the evening star was now brightly beaming, the mother turned a look of unspeakable affection on her boy and fervently kissed his forehead, with the admonition that he had better retire, as he had to be up betimes in the morning to start upon his journey, which both felt to be one of the most momentous events in his history.

Mary Temple was the widow of John Temple, a faithful Methodist minister, about twelve months deceased. In consequence of the long journeys, exposure to inclement weather, and the privation of comforts in the humble homes of the settlers among whom for years he had zealously laboured, his health, never robust, gave way. On one of his extensive rounds of preaching and visitation he was put to sleep in a cold and damp room—a not uncommon event with a pioneer preacher. Before he reached home he was in a violent fever. On partial convalescence he again resumed his work, only to be permanently laid aside. It was the great grief of his life to give up his life-work. As with hectic flush on his cheek and interrupted by a racking cough he " stated his case " before his brethren at the Conference, his emotions almost overcame him; but with the unquestioning faith of a Christian he bowed to the will of God.

He retired to Thornville, a village on the banks of the noble St. Lawrence, where he had invested his meagre savings in a few acres of land. It had been his first circuit. Here he had wooed and won and wedded the noble wife who had been such a faithful helpmate during the years of his itinerant toil—never flinching from trial, never repining at privation, ever cheering and supporting his own somewhat despondent spirit by her buoyancy of soul, her cheerful courage, her saintly piety, and her unfaltering faith.

As John Temple wrung, with an eager and feverish pressure but with speechless lips, the hands of his old companions in toil and travel as he left the Conference, few expected that they would ever see him again in the flesh. Yet for two years longer he survived, devoting himself chiefly to the education of his four children, and, with the help of his boys, to the cultivation of his few acres, too small to be called a farm, and rather large for a garden. As health permitted he preached in the neighbourhood, and always with great acceptance, for his character was beloved and revered, although his abilities were not brilliant and he was no longer in his prime.

The chief dependence of this family of six was the annual grant from the Superannuated Fund of their Church. The amount was not much—less than three hundred dollars in all,—but to those who had almost nothing else it was of inestimable value. Without its aid they would have suffered from abject poverty. Sometimes the expected grant—all too small at best—was subject to a considerable reduction. Then there was keen disappointment, but no complaining. The wife's faded dress was turned and worn over again. The threadbare coat was made to do longer service. With patient, loving industry the father's cast-off clothes were cut down and made over for the boys, the mother's for the girls. The coveted new book—a rarely purchased luxury, although the 'invalid was a man of studious tastes—was altogether dispensed with.

But growing, healthy, active boys and girls must have boots and shoes ; their clothing, unlike that of the Israelites during their wanderings in the Wilderness, *would* " wax old " and wear out ; and they were blessed with appetites of keenest zest. The energy and skill of the wise and loving house-mother were therefore taxed to the utmost to make ends meet ; and though she often had an anxious heart, she always wore a cheerful face, and no murmurings or repinings escaped her patient lips. The children were brought up in habits of thrift, economy, and self-denial, which are worth more than a fortune ; and a spirit of mutual helpfulness was fostered which made even poverty a blessing.

Still, the flour sometimes got low in the barrel, and the little stock of money very small in the purse, and sometimes it altogether failed. At such times the mother remained longer than usual in the little chamber, on whose table lay the well-used Bible, which was the daily food of her spiritual life; "Wesley's Hymns," with which, singing as she worked, she beguiled her daily household tasks; Bunyan's Pilgrim's Progress, the Lives of Mrs. Fletcher, Hester Ann Rogers, and other religious biographies and devotional works with which she occupied her scanty leisure. She always came out of this chamber with a deepened serenity upon her countenance; sometimes there were marks of tears on her face, but more often it shone with a holy light, as if, like Moses, she had been talking with God face to face.

Although the family was sometimes reduced to the last loaf and the last dollar, it never suffered actual want. In some unforeseen way their more pressing necessities were met. Sometimes a bag of flour, or of potatoes, or a ham was left at nightfall in the porch ; and more than once a five-dollar bill came in a letter without any name attached. Evidently among the sick pastor's friends were some who

"Did good by stealth, and blushed to find it fame."

These anonymous gifts were accepted without any sense of humiliation, as if they came direct from God Himself. While they formed slight ground of dependence, they fostered the faith of the inmates of the little cottage. Kindly neighbours, too, in that generous spirit which pervades almost all Canadian rural communities, after the first snow-fall made a " bee," and, with much shouting and " haw-geeing," hauled a great pile of logs into the yard for fuel. Many of these, however, were of such huge proportions as to employ most of the spare energies of the boys during the winter to reduce them to a usable size, thus developing at once their muscles and their industrial habits. At Christmas and New Year, too, more than one fat goose or turkey found its way in some mysterious manner to the minister's larder.

At one time, indeed, the faith of the heroic wife was sorely tried. For months her husband's health had been rapidly failing. At length he was confined entirely to bed, suffering much, and requiring constant medical attendance. The extra comforts his condition required had used up all the money available. The winter came on early and severe. Every resource but prayer was exhausted; and with increased fervour the faithful wife addressed herself to the Throne of Grace. When things seemed at their uttermost extremity relief came. In the dusk of one bleak evening a waggon drove up to the back-door of the humble cottage, loaded with an abundant supply of meat, flour, vegetables, a web of cloth to make dresses for the girls and their mother, and a sufficient quantity of stouter material for the boys. A kind note expressed the sympathies of the neighbours for the sick minister, accompanied by the sum of twenty dollars in money and a receipt in full of the doctor's and druggist's account. The good doctor was evidently the moving spirit in the generous and thoughtful donation. It was not the first time that he had ministered to the necessities of those of his patients who were poor in this world's goods. Like a chestnut burr, beneath a rugged exterior he concealed a sweet and mellow-heart.

It would have more than compensated the kind

donors of these gifts if they could have seen the rapt
expression of gratitude on the face of the worn and
weary wife, and heard the invalid faintly falter out
the words of Holy Writ : "I have been young, and
now am old; yet have I not seen the righteous
forsaken, nor his seed begging bread."

At length the last scene came. The sick man sank
lower and lower till he could scarce articulate.
Although leaving his wife and children almost without a dollar in the world, his mind seemed undisturbed
by doubt or anxiety on their behalf.

"Be careful for nothing," he whispered in the ear
of his sorrow-stricken wife, who sat by his bedside ;
"but in every thing by prayer and supplication with
thanksgiving let your requests be made known unto
God."

Again, she heard him softly whispering to himself
the blessed promises, "Leave thy fatherless children,
I will preserve them alive ; and let thy widows trust
in Me ; " "In Thee the fatherless findeth mercy ;"
and, "A Father of the fatherless, and a Judge of the
widows, is God in His holy habitation."

"O, wife ! " he whispered, when he saw her beside
him, "God never shows His fatherliness so much as
when He promises to be a Husband of the widow and
a Father of the fatherless. I leave you and the dear
children in His hands. He will do more and better
for you than you can either ask or think. Cast all
your care on Him. 'Trust in the Lord, and do good ;
so shalt thou dwell in the land, and verily thou shalt
be fed.' "

The weeping children he called to his side, and,
placing his weak hands on their heads, gave them his
blessing. He bade them love their mother, love their
Saviour, and prepare to meet him—their father—in
heaven.

"Lawrence, my boy," he whispered, gazing with a
look of ineffable affection on the face of his first-born,

" you are consecrated from your birth. If God calls
you to walk in my footsteps, He will be all to you
that He has been to me. My dying prayer is that
you may be the King's Messenger to dying men—
that our house may never want a man to stand before
the Lord."

"It won't be long," he whispered after a pause,
"till we shall all be gathered home. I know, I feel
certain," he continued in the full assurance of faith,
"that not one shall be left behind—that we shall all
be bound up in the bundle of life, an unbroken family
in heaven. 'Bless the Lord, O my soul, and forget
not all'"——but the remainder of the doxology was
uttered in heaven. His face grew radiant, he half
rose from his pillow,

"Sweet was the light of his eyes, but it suddenly sank into
darkness,
As when a lamp is blown out by a gust of wind at a casement."

He fell back on the arm of his weeping wife. On
his countenance rested a look of ineffable peace, as if
he had indeed seen the King in His beauty and the
land that is very far off. He was not, for God had
taken him.

That parting scene Lawrence Temple never forgot.
Often in dreams he lived that hour over again, and as
he woke from sleep he seemed to feel his father's hand
laid in blessing on his head, and to hear his father's
voice summoning him to be the King's messenger to
dying men. A sense of responsibility rested upon him.
He became almost a father to his brother and sisters,
and to his widowed mother more than a son.

Never were the benefits of Christian sympathy more
marked than in the kind and generous assistance of
the neighbours on the death of the minister. The
income of the widow from the Superannuated Fund
was a good deal lessened, but loving hearts and kind
hands provided for the immediate wants of the family.

For Lawrence was procured the village school, of which
he proved a highly successful teacher. His mother,
whose courageous soul had sustained her husband
during his long illness, now seemed to lean on the
brave heart and strong will of her first-born. A look
of manly gravity settled on his countenance, but a
chivalric deference, an almost lover-like tenderness,
marked his every act and word toward his mother.

While he taught others in the school, an unquench-
able thirst for knowledge possessed his own soul. He
nourished the project in his mind of going to college,
although there seemed no possibility of the accomplish-
ment of his desire. He found, however, that he could
earn more by the labour of his hands than by the
labour of his brain. He therefore, with the consent
of the school trustees, transferred his office of teacher
to his sister Mary, two years younger than himself,
whom he had diligently " coached " for the duties of
the office. Through the interest of a friend of his
father's at Montreal, he procured the promise of a
place in a " crew " of lumbermen operating on the
upper waters of the Ottawa. Our story opens on the
eve of his departure. His little hand-valise was
already packed. It contained, beside his slender
stock of under-clothing, every stitch of which was
enfibred with a mother's love, his father's Bible and
Greek Testament, a Latin Psalter, and his mother's
copy of " Wesley's Hymns." His sister Mary had
given him her favourite and almost her only book
of poetry, a tiny copy of Keble's " Christian Year."
His brother Tom gave him a handsome knife, earned
by running errands after school hours for the village
store. And little Nellie, the curly-headed pet of the
household, had netted for him a purse, which was
more than sufficiently large for his slender stock of
money—only a few shillings—with which he was
leaving home to win his fortune in the world. The
love-gifts of the poor, often procured with much self-

denial and sacrifice, may be intrinsically of little worth, but they convey a world of affection, which the easily-purchased presents of the rich cannot always express.

The household were up early in the morning. The coffee, prepared by the mother's loving hands, never had a richer aroma, nor the wheaten cakes a finer flavour. The girls tried to disguise their feelings by sundry admonitions to their brother concerning the fascinations of some Indian Minnehaha, whose subtile wiles they seemed to fear ; and Tom exhorted him to be sure and bring him home a bearskin rug. The mother said little, but wistfully watched through gathering tears the face of her son as he ostentatiously *seemed* to be eagerly eating the breakfast for which he had, in truth, little appetite. At length the stage horn blew and the lumbering vehicle rattled up to the door. Hurried leave-taking followed—except a lingering embrace between mother and son—and he was soon whirled away from their midst. The mother that day remained longer than usual in her chamber, and when she came out the mark of secret tears was on her face.

CHAPTER II.

AN UNEXPECTED FRIEND.

"Thine own friend, and thy father's friend, forsake not."
Prov. xxvii. 10.

OUR young knight was now fairly in the saddle, metaphorically, that is, and in quest of fortune. His prospects were not very brilliant; but he had a brave heart and a noble purpose within, two things that will take a man anywhere and enable him to do anything. They are akin to the faith that will remove mountains. He had first a long and weary stage ride to the town of Ottawa (it was before the time of railways in that part of Canada of which we write). At the close of the second day the stage toiled slowly up the long hill on which the town is situated, threw off its mail bags at the post-office, and drew up at a noisy tavern, before which creaked and groaned in the wind a swinging sign bearing the effigy of the Sheaf and Crown. The place reeked with tobacco smoke and the fumes of liquor, and loud and profane talking filled the air. Lawrence tried to close his senses to the vile sights and sounds and smells, and modestly asked for supper and a bed.

"What'll you have to drink?" asked the red-faced bar-tender of whom he made the inquiry, expectorating

PARLIAMENT BUILDINGS, OTTAWA.

WHEN THE STEW WAS READY, THE COOK BLEW A TIN HORN.—*Page 22.*

a discharge of tobacco juice into the huge spittoon in the middle of the floor.

"Thank you, I don't drink," replied Lawrence.

"O! you won't take nuthin', won't yer? You're one of the pious sort, I 'low," answered the bar-tender, with a contemptuous sneer on his vulgar face ; and turning away to mix drinks for two burly fellows in red flannel shirts, he tossed his thumb over his shoulder to indicate the way to the dining-room.

Lawrence sat down at a table covered with a crumpled and gravy-stained cloth, supporting a rickety cruet and some chipped and cracked dishes, when a bold-faced girl, with great gilt earrings and with a stare that made him blush to the tips of his ears, asked him what he would have. Unused to ordering his meals, he modestly replied that he would take whatever was convenient. With an ill-bred giggle she brought him a meal which only his keen hunger enabled him to eat. Presently the red-shirted fellows came from the bar-room and familiarly ordered their supper. From their rough talk Lawrence discovered that they were lumberers on their way, like himself, to the lumber camps. He made some casual inquiry as to the distance to the Mattawa River, on which the camp to which he was bound was situated.

"A matter of two hundred miles or so," replied one of the men.

"Be you goin' thar, stranger?" asked the other.

Lawrence replied that he was, when he of the red shirt continued, in an accent that indicated that he was from the forests of Maine,—

"Wal now, want ter know! Be you clerkin' it?"

Our hero replied that he was going as either axeman or teamster, with both of which employments he said he was familiar. Indeed he had acquired considerable dexterity in both at home.

"What on 'arth be the like o' ye going to do up thar?" exclaimed the man, as he stared at the thin white hands and slender, well-dressed person of the boy.

" O, I'll make my way as others have done before me," said Lawrence.

" Wal, ye've got pluck, any way ; and thet's all a man wants to get on enywheers, so fer's I see," said the good-natured fellow, as Lawrence bowed politely and rose from the table.

" Gentlemanly sort o' coot, isn't he ? " continued the lumberman *sotto voce* to his comrade.

" He'll soon git enough of the camp, or I'm mistaken," answered that worthy ; which remark, overheard by Lawrence, did not prove particularly inspiriting.

In order to escape the unsavoury odours and uncongenial company of the bar, which seemed to be the only public sitting-room in the house, Lawrence retired to the small, close, and stuffy chamber assigned him. Opening the window for fresh air, he saw in the distance, gleaming in the moonlight, the shining reaches of the river.

" There lies my destiny," he said to himself, as he gazed up the majestic stream which seemed to beckon him onward to the mysterious unknown regions beyond. He thought of the brave explorer Champlain, who, first of white men, had traversed that gleaming track and penetrated the far recesses of the Canadian wilderness ; and of Brebeuf, and Lalemant, and Davost, and Daniel, the intrepid Jesuit missionaries who, two hundred years before, for the love of souls, had toiled up the tortuous stream, sleeping on the bare rock, carrying their burdens over the frequent and rugged portages, till they reached their far-off Indian mission on the shores of the " Sweet Water Sea," as they called the vast and billowy expanse of Lake Huron. There three of these four had suffered a cruel martyrdom ; rejoicing that they were counted worthy to confess Christ among the heathen and to glorify God by their sufferings and death. The memory of the faith and patience of these early Canadian martyrs, although of an alien race and creed, enbraved the heart of this Canadian youth, two centuries after their death, to pursue the path of duty in the face of whatever obstacles might rise.

Then his eye fell upon the evening star, beaming with a lambent flame low down in the sky, still warm with the after-glow of the departed sun, and gentler thoughts rose within his breast. Only two nights before he had gazed upon it by his mother's side. She was probably gazing on it now, and, he was certain, thinking of him and praying for him. The steady glow of the star seemed like the light of his mother's eyes beaming in blessing upon him, and in the sense of spiritual communion with home and the loved ones there, he forgot his squalid surroundings and their contrast with the sweet, clean comforts of his mother's roof. Praying to his Father Who seeth in secret, he felt that he was not alone, for God was with him.

"Thine own friend, and thy father's friend, forsake not."
Prov. xxvii. 10.

With the earliest dawn Lawrence was abroad to breathe the fresh air, and to learn where he could find the "crew" of lumbermen he was about to join. Just as the sun rose, he reached the cliff known as Government Hill, now crowned by the stately and many-turreted Parliament Buildings of the Dominion of Canada. As the sun rose grandly over the far-rolling Laurentian hills, it turned the river into gleaming gold. Beneath the cliff, shagged with ancient woods from top to base, sparkled and dimpled the eddies of the rapid stream. Acres of timber rafts were moored in the cove, and in the still morning air the thin blue smoke of the camp fires rose where the raftsmen were preparing their morning meal.

While he gazed in admiration on the scene, he became aware of a grizzled, sun-browned man, with a

kindly grey eye, and dressed in a sort of half-sailor
garb, standing beside him.

"Kinder nice, that 'ere, ain't it now?" said the
stranger.

"It is, indeed, very beautiful," replied Lawrence.

"I've lived on this river, man an' boy, well nigh
on to fifty years, an' I hain't got tired on it yet. It
don't never wear out, ye see. It's new every mornin',
an' renewed every evenin', like all the rest of the
Good Bein's blessin's."

Encouraged by the kindly look and pious tone of the
old man, Lawrence asked him if he knew where Hargrave's crew of lumbermen were camped (this was the
name of his employer).

"Hargrave's crew! I should think I'd oughter. I
supplies 'em most o' their campin' outfit. Ye see that
smoke," he said, pointing to the spray rising from the
Chaudiere Falls; "well, that's the Big Kittle. Jist
around the p'int beyond that ye'll find Hargrave's
camp. They break up and go up stream to-day. You
jist ask for Mike Callaghan at the bridge there, an'
he'll tell you exactly the way."

Lawrence took out his note-book to write down the
name, when a piece of paper fluttered to the ground.
The old man stooped to pick it up, and was handing
it to Lawrence when he exclaimed,—

"What's this? A class-ticket, as I'm alive! Where
did ye get this, boy? Are ye a Methodis'?" abruptly
asked the old man.

"Yes, I am a Methodist," said Lawrence, "and
I got this from James Turner, our minister at Thornville."

"Turner! I know'd him," exclaimed our ancient
mariner; "was on this circuit once. I must know
your name, lad."

Willing to humour his strange companion, Lawrence
mentioned his name, the utterance of which produced
a remarkable effect. With a quick motion the old

man grasped him firmly by the shoulder and peered earnestly into his face, and then exclaimed, " Well-a-day ! an' to think I didn't know ye ! "

" I see nothing very remarkable in that," replied Lawrence, " since you never saw me before."

" Don't be so sure o' that, my boy ; I know'd ye afore ye know'd yerself, and well I know'd yer father, too. I see his looks in your very face. How is he, anyway ? " rattled on the old sailor.

" He is dead these twelve months," said Lawrence, with a gush of sympathy towards the man who had known his father.

" Dead, is it ? " exclaimed the stranger in a tone of mingled astonishment and grief. " An' old Jimmie Daily left, who could be so much better spared. Well, a good man is gone to his reward—rest his soul ! "— Mr. Daily, although now a Methodist, in moments of excitement occasionally used expressions with which he was familiar while yet a Roman Catholic.

" How long since you knew my father ? " asked Lawrence, now deeply interested.

" Knew him, is it ? It's well nigh twenty years agone," he answered. " Many's the time I ferried him across the river down at Metcalf's appointment—the ould log church, do ye mind ? An' the ways he used to talk to me ! I was a sinful man in those days, God forgive me, but I never forgot thim words ; an' he made me promise to go to the praichin', an' I kep' my word, but I soon wished I hadn't, for he made me feel my sins that bad that I couldn't slape, an' I tuk to the drink harder nor ever, an' I got the horrors, an' he watched with me like a brother, an' tuk me to his own house to keep me from the tavern, an' prayed an' wrasled with me till I got my soul converted. Halle-lujah !

' O happy day, that fixed my choice ! '

So ye're a son of John Timple, God bless ye ; an' yer

2

mother, is she livin'? If ever there was a saint, it was that woman. An' where are ye stoppin'?"

"At the Sheaf and Crown," replied Lawrence; and he briefly told of his father's illness and his mother's welfare.

"At the Sheaf and Crown, is it?" the garrulous old man went on. Well, ye'll stop there no longer. It's no place for the likes o' ye. A proud man will be Jimmie Daily to entertain the son of his best friend, John Timple. Come home to breakfast with me."

Nothing loath to leave the tavern, Lawrence cheerfully accepted the warm-hearted hospitality of his Irish friend. The old man was a widower, but his two daughters, bright-eyed but bashful girls, had a clean and appetizing breakfast ready, to which Lawrence did ample justice.

"An' what way are ye goin' now, if I may make so bould?" asked Mr. Daily towards the close of the meal.

"To the River Mattawa, with Hargrave's crew," quietly answered Lawrence.

"To the Mattawa!" exclaimed the kind host in amazement, dropping his knife and fork and staring at his guest with open-mouthed astonishment. "Och, it's jokin' an ould man ye are. But it'll be gunnin' or fishin' ye're after?"

His astonishment deepened as Lawrence avowed his purpose to go as a lumberman, at the same time hinting that it was only a temporary expedient for a special purpose. At length he went on:

"That's not the kind o' work for John Timple's son, that I nursed when he was a baby. An' ye don't look over strong, naythur. But ye've got yer father's sperit. Nothin' ever did beat that man. No matter what roads or weather, I never know'd him to miss an app'intment, an' the roads wuz powerful bad sometimes. But I won't say ye nay. I'm sure Providence will direct ye. But come here, my boy," he said, rising from the table and leading the way into the little store which was his chief source of livelihood.

It was an odd miscellaneous assortment of articles that almost filled the little apartment. Three sides of the room were appropriated respectively to groceries, dry goods, and hardware. But this distinction was not rigidly maintained, and sundry articles would not come under any of these heads, as, for instance, Bibles, hymn-books, school-books and stationery, a case of patent medicines, and oils, paints, and brushes. The windows occupying the fourth side were filled with specimens of the different kinds of goods on the shelves. From the ceiling hung steel traps, log-chains, snowshoes, moccasins, and iron-studded boots for raftsmen. Cant-hooks, axes, whips, harness, row-locks, trolling-lines, fish-hooks, rope, cordage, codfish, molasses, sugar, tea, coffee, mess-pork and mess-beef, pea-jackets, sou'-westers, oil-cloth pilot-coats, thick guernseys, blankets, mits, fur caps, mufflers—almost every thing one could think of, or that lumbermen could want, from a grindstone to a needle, from a herring to a barrel of flour, from linen thread to hawsers, from handkerchiefs to sail-cloth, was represented in this " general store."

Selecting two stout guernsey shirts, a pair of moccasins and a pair of boots, a blanket and a pair of buckskin mits, Mr. Daily quietly made them up in a parcel, saying, " Ye'll find the need of thim before the winter is over."

In vain Lawrence remonstrated, and protested that he could not afford to buy, and did not want to acccept as a gift, these valuable articles.

" Is it sell the likes o' thim to yer father's son ye'd have me ? " exclaimed the generous-hearted creature in affected indignation. " Not if I knows it. It's more than this I owe the memory of John Timple, or to any that bear his name."

He then conducted his young *protégé*, in whom he

seemed to take paternal pride, to the camp which was the rendezvous of Hargrave's brigade. The "crew," as it was called, was busy with the fiual bustle of embarking on their six or eight months' plunge into the wilderness. There was no time for many words. Commending Lawrence to the foreman or "boss" of the brigade, as the "son of a dear ould friend," the old man gave his hand a wring like the grip of a vice, with the valediction—

"God bless ye, my boy, and all the saints protect ye."

CHAPTER III.

ON THE RIVER.

" V'là l'bon vent !
V'là l'joli vent !
V'là l'bon vent !
Ma mie m'appelle !

V'là l'bon vent !
V'là l'joli vent !
V'là l'bon vent !
Ma mie m'attend ! " *

IT was a picturesque scene that met the eyes of Lawrence when he had time to look around him. The broad river was flashing and eddying in the bright sunlight, rushing on to the Chaudière Falls, like a strong will bent on a desperate resolve. This brilliant picture was framed by a dark background of pines —a fringe of shivering aspens near the water in some places trailing their branches in the current like Naiads bathing their tresses in the waves. Moored in a little cove were a number of stout bateaux, and several birch bark canoes were drawn up upon the shore. Nearly a hundred men, with much shouting and gesticulation, were loading the bateaux with

* For this refrain, the burden of a popular *voyageurs'* chorus, we are indebted to our friend, W. Kirby, Esq., the author of that remarkably clever Canadian story, " The *Chien d'Or.*"

barrels of mess-pork and mess-beef, flour, sugar, and molasses; boxes of tea and tobacco; bales of blankets, and all the almost countless necessaries of a lumber camp. The lumbermen were sun-tanned, stalwart fellows, many of whom were French Canadian, and the others of different nationalities, including three or four Indians. Almost all wore red-flannel shirts, and many had a scarlet sash around the waist and a red woven cap or fez upon their heads.

A camp-fire was blazing brightly on the beach, at which a grimy-looking cook, with a short and dirty tobacco-pipe in his mouth, was preparing dinner in sundry smoke-blackened vessels. When the stew of meat and vegetables was ready, he blew a tin horn, and the captains of the several messes received their shares in large tin vessels. These distributed in tin dishes to the men of their messes their portion of meat in due season. Strong green tea, without milk, was the only beverage furnished.

In an incredibly short time dinner was despatched, and almost every man produced a tobacco-pipe, and was soon smoking away like a small furnace. The last loads were hurried on board the bateaux. The oars were manned, and with a cheer the several crews rowed their boats up the stream, hugging the shore as closely as possible in order to avoid the strength of the current. The canoes were launched and went dancing over the waves, the "boss" and the Indians going ahead to select and prepare the camping ground.

Lawrence took his place at the oar in one of the bateaux, and rowed lustily with the rest of the crew. He greatly enjoyed his novel experience. He had a keen eye for the picturesque, and now he found much to employ it. The flood of golden light on the broad bosom of the river, the vivid green of the foliage on the shore, the bronzed faces, often full of character, and the stalwart forms of his red-shirted companions, the brown bateaux and the snowy sails, which were spread to catch the light breeze which helped them along—these made up a picture that, transferred to canvas, would have won an artist fame and fortune.

He cordially cultivated the acquaintance of his fellow-oarsman, a good-natured Frenchman, clad in a strange blending of civilized and savage attire. He wore buck-skin leggings, fringed after the Indian style, bead-worked moccasins, a red sash, red shirt, and red night-cap or fez. Around his forehead was a band of wampum, or Indian beadwork, set off by a heron's plume, dyed red. In his belt, in a leathern scabbard, was a sharp and glittering scalping-knife, which, however, he used for no more deadly purpose than cutting his meat and tobacco. On one finger he wore a solid gold ring, and in his ears small earrings of the same material. A silver cross and a scapular of the Virgin might be seen on his bronzed breast through the open bosom of his shirt.

Jean Baptiste la Tour, such was his name, was a characteristic example of the *voyageurs* and *coureurs du bois* who, ever since the settlement of Canada by the French, had found the fascinations of the wild forest life too strong to permit them to remain in the precincts of civilization or engage in any steady agricultural labour. Lawrence found him very chatty, and as he could speak a little English and Lawrence a little book French, they got on very well together.

Baptiste had wandered all over the great North and North-West, as far as Fort Churchill on Hudson's Bay and up the Saskatchewan to near the foot of the Rocky Mountains. He had been employed by the Hudson's Bay Company in the varied avocations of trapper, *voyageur,* and guide ; but on one of his trips from Fort William, on Lake Superior, down the Ottawa to Montreal, with a convoy of furs, he had fallen a victim to the fascinations of a bright-eyed Indian girl at Caughnawaga. He had now a bark wigwam and squaw and two papooses at that village, and confined

his wanderings within a limit of some four hundred
miles, instead of two thousand as before.

He was full of vivacity, very polite in his way, somewhat choleric and hasty when crossed, and a rather
boastful talker, He was very proud of his aristocratic
ancestry. He claimed descent from the Chevalier de
la Tour, Governor of Acadie in the seventeenth century,
and favoured Lawrence with highly romantic traditions
of the beauty and valour and fidelity to her husband's
chequered fortunes of the heroic Madame de la Tour,
narrating how she held the fort at the mouth of the
St. John against threefold odds. The relationship
claimed was not improbable, for some of the best blood
of France, that of the Montforts and Montmorencis,
flowed in the veins of semi-savage wanderers in the
woods or dwellers in Indian wigwams.

Towards evening the brigades of boats swept into
a little cove, where, behind a narrow beach, the dense
foliage rose like a castle wall. A little streamlet
shily trickled down, making timid music over its
pebbles. In an open space the camp-fires were soon
blazing brightly, the splendid black and brown bass,
caught by trolling in the river, were soon broiling on
the coals, and never lordly feast at a king's table was
enjoyed with keener zest than the frugal repast of these
hardy lumbermen.

It was soon dark, for the season was September, and,
in the light of the camp-fires, the lounging figures
smoking their short pipes, and some, we are sorry to
say, playing cards, looked like a group of bandits in
one of Salvator Rosa's paintings. The trees overhead
gleamed in the firelight like fretted silver, and through
the rifts the holy stars looked down like sentinels in
mail of burnished steel keeping ward upon the walls
of heaven.

Leaving the uncongenial company, Lawrence plunged
into the caves of darkness of the grand old forest,
which lifted on pillared colonnades its interlaced and

fretted roof, more stately and awe-inspiring in the
gloom than any minster aisle. There, with thoughts
of home and God and heaven, he strengthened his
heart for the duties and the trials of his new life.

On returning to the camp he gratefully accepted
the invitation of the foreman to share his tent, and
soon, lying on a bear-skin rug spread upon a bed of
fragrant spruce boughs, was fast asleep. The rest of
the crew threw themselves down in their blankets with
their feet to the fire, and slept beneath the open canopy
of heaven.

With the dawn the camp was astir. Breakfast was
promptly despatched, and as the sun rose, turning the
waters into gleaming gold, the little flotilla again
glided on its way. So passed day after day. Lawrence
was often weary in back and arms and legs with
rowing, and his hands were severely blistered; but
the ever-changing panorama of beauty was a perpetual
delight. Sometimes, as they approached a rapid in
the river, the sturdy boatmen would spring into the
water and push and drag the bateaux against the
foaming current. When the rapid was too strong to
be overcome in this way, the boats were lightened and
pushed up with poles, and dragged with ropes. The
bales and boxes, supported on the broad backs of the
men by a band going around their foreheads, were
carried over the portage to the calm water beyond.

The light-hearted Frenchmen beguiled their labour
by boat songs having a rattling chorus like that which
heads this chapter, in which all joined. The favourite
song was that of the king's son who went a-hunting
with his silver gun, with its strange reiteration and
stirring chorus, which made every rower spring to
his oar with renewed vivacity and vigour.

The following will be a sufficient specimen of this
national boat song of French Canada:

"Derrière chez nous y-a-t-un étang,
    En roulant ma boule.

Trois beaux canards s'en vont baignant,
  Rouli, roulant, ma boule roulant,
En roulant ma boule roulant,
  En roulant ma boule.
Trois beaux canards s'en vont baignant,
  En roulant ma boule.
Le fils du roi s'en va chassant,
  Rouli, etc.

Le fils du roi s'en va chassant,
  En roulant ma boule,
Avec son grand fusil d'argent,
  Rouli, etc.
Avec son grand fusil d'argent,
  En roulant ma boule.
Visa le noir, tua le blanc,
  Rouli, etc.
Visa le noir, tua le blanc,
  En roulant ma boule.
O fils du roi, tu es méchant,
  Rouli, etc."

So it goes on for thirteen verses, but of its simple melody the *voyageurs* never tire. Baptiste led the refrain, with infinite gusto, in a rich tenor voice, and the whole company, English and French, joined in the chorus, waking the echoes of the forest aisles and feathery crags as they passed. On all our Canadian streams, from the grand and gloomy Saguenay to the far Saskatchewan, this song has been chanted for over two hundred years. It is, therefore, as a relic of a phase of national life fast passing away, not unworthy of a place in this chronicle.

JEAN BAPTISTE, THE LIGHT-HEARTED
FRENCHMAN.

AMONG THE PINES.

CHAPTER IV.

THE LUMBER CAMP.

"A man was famous according as he had lifted up axes upon the thick trees."—Psalm lxxiv. 5.

"How bowed the woods beneath their sturdy stroke!"
GRAY'S *Elegy.*

AT length the little flotilla reached the Mattawa river. A heavy boom of floating logs chained together was moored across its mouth to intercept timber coming down its stream. An opening was made in this, and, proceeding a short distance, the brigade reached at last its destination. A camp had occupied the ground the previous season, and the buildings were still standing, although one had been partially unroofed by a summer storm.

The camp consisted of three buildings forming three sides of a hollow square, the fourth side being open, with a warm sunny southern exposure, toward the river. To the right was a strongly-built storehouse for keeping the flour, pork, tea, sugar, and other supplies required for a hundred men for half a year. To the left were the stables for the ten or twelve teams which were daily expected to arrive by a trail along the river side through the forest.

The third side of the square was occupied by "the

shanty " or boarding-house for the men. Instead of
being, as its name might imply, a frail structure, it
was a large, strongly-built log-house. The openings
between the logs were filled with moss and clay. The
windows were very few and small. For this there
were three reasons—larger openings would weaken the
structure of the house, and let in more cold, and
glass was a rather scarce commodity on the Mattawa.

The whole interior was one large room. The most
conspicuous object was a huge log fireplace or platform, like an ancient altar, in the centre of the floor.
It was covered with earth and blackened embers, and
was surrounded by a protecting border of cobble stones.
Immediately over it an opening in the roof gave vent
to the smoke, although in dull weather much of it
lingered among the rafters, which fact gave them a
rather sombre appearance. Around the wall were rude
" bunks " or berths like those in a ship, for the accommodation of the shantymen. A few exceedingly
solid-looking benches, tables, and shelves, made with
backwoodsman skill with no other instrument than
an axe and auger, was all the furniture visible. Some
wooden pegs were driven in the wall to support the
guns, powder-horns, shot-pouches, and extra clothing
of the men. Over the doorway was fastened a large
deer's head with branching antlers. The house was
warm and comfortable, but with nothing like privacy
for the men.

The other buildings were similarly constructed and
roofed with logs split and partially hollowed out.
During the fine weather the cooking was done at a
camp-fire in the courtyard, but in winter at the huge
hearth in the shanty. A large log hollowed into a
trough caught rain water, while for culinary purposes
a spring near at hand sufficed.

On the walls of the stable were stretched out, dried
by the sun, stained by the weather and torn by the
wind, the skins of several polecats, weasels, and other

vermin, evidence of the prowess of the stable boys and a warning of the fate which awaited all similar depredators—just as the Danish pirates, when captured by the Saxons, were flayed and their skins nailed to the church doors, as a symbol of the stern justice meted out in the days of the Heptarchy.

A couple of hardy Scotch squatters had cleared a patch of ground near the camp, and raised a crop of oats, and cured a quantity of wild meadow hay, for which they got a good price from the lumber company.

The deserted camp was soon in a bustle of activity, and the abandoned buildings were promptly re-occupied. The stores were safely housed and padlocked. Each man stowed away his "kit" under his berth or on a shelf or peg above it. Axes were sharpened on a large grindstone, and when necessary fitted with new helves, and every one was prepared for a winter campaign against the serried array of forest veterans. Such are the general arrangements adopted for carrying out the great national industry of Canada —an industry in which more capital is employed than in any other branch of business, and from which a greater annual revenue is derived.

The day after the arrival of the lumber crew at the camp, Lawrence was told off with a "gang" of men to proceed a short distance up the stream and begin the work of felling trees. The air was cool and bracing, and fragrant with pine balm. The stately trunks rose like a pillared colonnade, "each fit to be the mast of some high admiral." The pine needles made an elastic carpet under foot, and the bright sunlight streamed down through the openings of the forest, flecking the ground with patches of gold.

Soon the assigned limit was reached, and the stalwart axe-men each selected his antagonist in this life-and-death duel with the ancient monarchs of the forest. The scanty brushwood was cleared. The axes gleamed brightly in the air The measured strokes

fell thick and fast, awaking strange echoes in the
dim and distant forest aisles. The white chips flew
through the air, and ghastly wounds gaped in the
trunks of the ancient pines. Now a venerable forest
chief shivered through all his branches, swayed for
a moment in incertitude, like blind Ajax fighting with
his unseen foe, then, with a shuddering groan, tottered and reeled, crashing down, shaking the earth
and air in his fall. As he lay there, a prostrate giant
that had wrestled with the storms of a hundred
winters, felled by the hand of man in a single hour,
the act seemed like murder. As Lawrence stood with
his foot on the fallen trunk of his first tree, but a
moment before standing grand and majestic and lordly
as a king's son, like Saul among the prophets, he
seemed guilty of sacrilege—of slaying the Lord's
anointed. He followed in fancy its fate:

" Mid shouts and cheers
The jaded steers,
Panting beneath the goad,
Drag down the weary winding road
Those captive kings so straight and tall,
To be shorn of their streaming hair,
And, naked and bare,
To feel the stress and the strain
Of the wind and the reeling main,
Whose roar
Would remind them for evermore
Of their native forests they should not see again."

But after a time his conscience became seared and
callous to this tree murder, and as he swung his
glittering axe through the air and it bit deep into the
very heart of some grand old pine, stoical beneath his
blows as a forest sachem under the knife of his enemy,
a stern joy filled his soul, as he felt that he with that
tiny weapon was more than a match for the towering
son of Anak. It realized the fairy tales of his boyhood, and he played the *rôle* of Jack the Giant-killer
over again.

LOADING UP THE LOGS.

HAULING LOGS ON THE ICE.

The fallen trees were cut into logs of suitable
length by huge saws worked by a couple of brawny
sawyers. When the snow fell, these were drawn to
the river side by sturdy teams of oxen. The logs
were loaded on the sleds by being rolled up an
inclined plane formed by a pair of "skids." A
stout chain was attached to the sled and passed around
the log, and a pair of oxen tugged at the other end of
the chain till the unwieldy mass, sometimes weigh-
ing nearly a ton, was hauled on to the sled. This
heavy work, as may be supposed, is not without
danger ; and sometimes serious accidents occur, when
only the rude surgery of the foreman or "boss" is
available.

But although Lawrence, like a strong-limbed warrior,
thus "drank the joy of battle with his peers," he often
also felt the warrior's fatigue, and sometimes the
warrior's peril and wounds. One day a tree in falling
struck the projecting branch of another and dashed it
to the ground in dangerous proximity to his person,
and a portion of it, rebounding, gave him a severe
blow on the leg. And at night as he laid his weary
limbs and aching joints upon the fragrant hemlock
boughs of his berth, his hot and blistered hands often
kept him awake, and he contrasted, not without a
pang, the quiet and neatness of his little attic chamber
beneath his mother's roof with the uncongenial surroundings by which he was environed. The frugal yet
clean and appetizing fare of his mother's table, with
its snowy cloth and dainty dishes, and, above all, her
saintly presence beaming with a sacred influence like
the seraphic smile of Murillo's Madonna, were remembered with a longing akin to that of the Israelites in
the desert for the fleshpots of Egypt, as he partook of
his mess of pork and beans or Irish stew, and drank
out of his tin pannikin his strong green tea, un-
flavoured with milk. Hunger, however, gave a zest to
his appetite, and the monotonous fare of the camp was

3

sometimes varied by the killing of a deer or the snaring of a covey of partridges.

Lawrence was not without spiritual contests also as well as conflicts with the giants of the forest, and the former were the more desperate and deadly of the two. To live a godly life amid all these godless men—for so far as he knew none of them had any personal experience of religion—was no slight task. To confess Christ humbly and modestly, yet boldly and firmly, amid his unfavourable surroundings taxed his Christian resolution.

It was not long before he had an opportunity of bearing the reproach of Christ. To a lad of his retiring and sensitive disposition it was quite an ordeal to observe his religious devotions at night and morning amid the smoking and foolish, and often profane, talking and jesting of nearly a hundred rude and boisterous men. On the journey up the river he had sought the solitude of the forest for his devotions. He could still have done so in the camp, but he thought that it would be an act of moral cowardice to conceal his habit of prayer. He therefore from the very first night read a chapter in his father's Bible, and knelt quietly beside his "bunk" to pray to his Father in heaven. This act had a salutary effect on those near him. Most of them either ceased their conversation or subdued their voices to a lower key. Those who would do neither moved away, as if reproached by his act. Indeed, some of the Roman Catholic lumbermen began to imitate his conduct, a few openly, and others turning to the wall and furtively crossing themselves before they retired to rest. The quiet dignity without haughty reserve, and the uniform politeness and kindness of the young man, had won the respect or good nature of most of the motley forest community.

One night a rough Irish teamster, Dennis O'Neal by name, came into the shanty in a decidedly ill humour.

He had been breaking in a yoke of young steers that the foreman had bought from the Scotch squatter—an employment not calculated to mollify a temper somewhat irascible at the best of times. He grumbled over his supper and quarrelled with the cook. As he caught sight of Lawrence kneeling at his bedside, he seemed to consider him a fitting object on which to vent his ill-humour. Picking up a musk rat which one of the Indians had killed and was going to cook for his private gratification, O'Neal hurled it at the head of Lawrence with the objurgation,

"Get up, ye spalpeen. What for are ye makin' yerself so much better than the rest av us? It's some runaway 'prentice ye are, for all yer foine manners, bad luck to ye!"

Though struck fairly on the side of the face by the noisome missile, Lawrence made no reply, but bowed his head still lower and lifted up his heart more fervently to God.

"D'ye hear me, ye concated gossoon?" cried O'Neal in a rage; and he was about to hurl his heavy boot at the boy.

"Let be le garçon," exclaimed Baptiste la Tour, who had taken a fancy to Lawrence, arresting the hand of the irate O'Neal. "What for you no pray votre self? Sure you much need."

"Why don't he pray right then?" said O'Neal, adopting the usual plea for persecution—a difference of religious creed. "Where's his ' Hail, Mary ' ? "

"Indian pray to Grand Manitou," replied the philosophical Frenchman, who seems to have been tinctured with a rationalistic spirit; "Catholique pray to Sainte Marie; Protestant pray to Marie's Son : all good. Let be le garcon."

"That's so," "Let the boy alone," "Go to bed, Dennis," echoed several of the shantymen; and seeing that his treatment of Lawrence was unpopular, O'Neal slunk off growling to his bunk.

CHAPTER V.

A SABBATH IN THE CAMP.

"O day most calm, most bright,
The fruit of this, the next world's bud,
The endorsement of supreme delight,
Writ by a Friend and with His blood ;
The couch of time, care's balm and bay :—
The week were dark, but for thy light:
Thy torch doth show the way."

GEORGE HERBERT.

BY general consent Lawrence suffered no more overt persecution for his practice of prayer. He was, however, made the object of many little annoyances by O'Neal, who cherished a petty spite towards him, and by others who felt reproved by his quiet yet open confession of Christ, and who resented his superiority of manner and character. For instance, he sometimes found salt furtively introduced into his tea, instead of sugar, or a handful of beechnuts placed in his bed, their sharp angles not being promotive of sound slumber. Sometimes, too, his axe would mysteriously be blunted or mislaid, and other articles would disappear for a time or, indeed, altogether. As he exhibited no spirit of resentment, however, much less of retaliation, as seemed to be expected, and was always cheerful and obliging, these one-sided jokes, at which nobody laughed, lost their charm to their perpetrators, and were discontinued. It takes two to make a quarrel, and there was no use in annoying a man who never seemed to be annoyed.

Lawrence found opportunities also of disarming prejudice and winning favour by his helpful and cordial disposition. One day O'Neal was in real difficulty and some peril from his steers, which under his domineering mode of management had proved refractory, and had severely crushed their driver between the clumsy cart, in which he was hauling hay from the meadow stacks to the barn, and a huge stump which stood in the rough bush road. Lawrence ran to his assistance. With a few kind words he pacified the enraged animals, and extricated Dennis from his danger. As he was a good deal bruised, Lawrence hastily threw off most of the load, helped the injured man into the cart, and drove him slowly to the shanty, and, with the assistance of Baptiste, carried him to his bunk.

The next day was Sunday, a day which often seemed the most tedious of the week in the camp. Lawrence sorely missed the Sabbath services to which he had been accustomed, and was greatly distressed at the desecration of the holy day, of which he was the involuntary witness. Many of the men lay in their berths or bunks, or lounged about the shanty, unkempt and half-dressed, a good part of the day. Some wandered in the woods with dog and gun. Others fished, bathed, or paddled in the river in their bark canoes. In the evening most of them talked, smoked, played cards, or mended their clothes in the shanty. Lawrence was wont to retire to the woods with his Bible and hymn-book, and hold a Sabbath service by himself in the leafy temple of Nature. In the evening he used to seek a quiet corner, not only on Sunday but on week-nights when not too tired, and slowly and with much difficulty he spelt his way through the Gospel of St. John in his father's Greek Testament.

On this Sunday, however, instead of going out he

remained in the shanty and prepared some toast and tea for O'Neal, who, unable to rise, lay tossing and moaning impatiently in his rude bed.

"It's very kind av ye, shure," said the sick man, "afther the ways I've trated ye, it is."

"O, never mind that!" said Lawrence. "You won't do it again, I'm sure."

"Troth an' I won't. True for ye, boy! It's ashamed av meself ye make me, entirely."

"Would you like me to read to you a bit?" asked Lawrence.

"'Deed ye may if ye loike. I'm no great hand at the readin', but I'll listen as quiet as a dumb cratur, if it plazes ye."

Gladly accepting this not very gracious permission, Lawrence brought his Bible, and after thinking what would be least likely to offend the prejudices of the rather choleric patient, he read the beautiful hymn of the Virgin, "My soul doth magnify the Lord." He then read the story of the marriage at Cana of Galilee, with its account of the reverence paid by Mary to her Divine Son.

"Is that the Blessed Vargin ye're readin' about?" asked O'Neal with some interest.

"Yes," said Lawrence.

"Shure, she was the good woman," replied his patient in a sort of expostulatory tone.

"Certainly," continued the reader, "the 'blessed among women' the Bible calls her."

"Does it now? the Protestant Bible?" asked Dennis with eagerness. "An' is that it ye're readin'? Shure they tould me it was a bad book. Read me some more av it, if ye plaze."

Lawrence read him the touching story of Calvary, and then repeated the beautiful *Stabat Mater*, that hymn of ages with its sweet refrain,

"Mary stood the cross beside."

Strange that that hymn of the Umbrian monk should be repeated six hundred years after his death in a lumber shanty in the backwoods of Canada.

Lawrence then repeated Wesley's beautiful hymn :

> " Come, ye weary sinners, come,
>   All who groan beneath your load,
> Jesus calls His wanderers home,
>   Hasten to your pardoning God.
> Come, ye guilty spirits, oppressed,
>   Answer to the Saviour's call :
> ' Come, and I will give you rest :
>   Come, and I will save you all.' "

As he recited slowly and with much feeling the last verse :

> " Burdened with a world of grief,
>   Burdened with our sinful load,
> Burdened with this unbelief,
>   Burdened with the wrath of God ;
> Lo ! we come to Thee for ease,
>   True and gracious as Thou art ;
> Now our groaning soul release,
>   Write forgiveness on our heart,"

a tear trickled down the bronzed face of the sick man, the first that he had shed for years, and his features twitched convulsively as he said,

" True for ye. Burdened enough I've been, and far enough I've wandered. If the Blessed Vargin 'ud only look on a poor wretch, p'r'aps I might repint afther all."

Gently and lovingly Lawrence urged him to look from the Virgin to her Divine Son for the forgiveness of sins and spiritual succour that He alone can impart.

As he was about to leave the sick man, he laid his hand on his fevered brow and asked him kindly if he felt better.

" It's powerful wake I am," said the grateful fellow, " but, thanks to yer kindness, I'm cruel aisy."

Taking this rather contradictory statement as it was meant, Lawrence retired to his secret oratory in

the woods to thank God that he had been enabled to
overcome evil with good.   As he walked in the dim
forest aisles in the flush of the departing day, he felt
that in the rude lumber shanty he had been able to
serve God no less acceptably than if he had worshipped
beneath cathedral dome.   In seeking to do good unto
others his own soul had been benefited and blessed.

A QUIET REACH OF RIVER.

BACKWOODS CANADIAN SAWMILL.

CHAPTER VL

THE OXFORD SCHOLAR.

> " A Clerke ther was of Oxenforde also,
> That unto logike hadde long ygo,
> As lene was his hors as is a rake,
> And he was not right fat I undertako ;
> But looked holwe, and thereto soberly.
> Ful thredbare was his overest courtepy,
> But all be that he was a philosophre,
> Yet hadde he but litel gold in cofre."
> CHAUCER—*Canterbury Tales.*

THAT evening Lawrence sat reading his Greek Testament by the light of a tallow dip fixed in a tin sconce on the wall so as better to illumine the room. Except to those in its immediate proximity it seemed indeed

> " No light, but rather darkness visible."

Laying down his book for a moment, he rose to give a drink of water to his friend—for such he now was —Dennis O'Neal.

When he returned he found that one of a group of men who had been shuffling a pack of greasy cards was looking over his book. He was a tall, dark, morose, sinister-looking man, with iron-grey hair and an unkempt grisly beard, and was smoking a short black pipe.

"Do you tell me you can read that?" he asked abruptly.

"Not much, I am sorry to say," replied Lawrence, reaching for his book, for he began to fear that he was about to be made the victim of another stupid "practical joke," which is generally only as much of a joke to its victim as stoning was to the poor frogs in the fable.

Matt Evans, for by that name the man was known, returned the book, and soon, throwing down his cards, came and sat down on the edge of the bunk beside Lawrence.

"Where did you get that book?" he asked.

"It was my father's," said Lawrence, feeling a little anxious about his treasure. "It was almost his last gift."

"Was he a clergyman?" asked Evans.

"He was a Methodist minister," was the reply.

"A Methodist minister! Do they read Greek?" exclaimed Evans in a tone of surprise. "I thought they were a set of illiterate nomads, prowling around the country."

"Many of them do," said Lawrence, with quiet dignity, "and some of them read Hebrew also. My father taught himself."

"It's many a year since I read any. Let's see if I have forgotten it all," said Evans.

"Where did you learn it?" asked Lawrence, handing him the Testament.

"Where they know how to teach it, my boy—at Oxford. I don't look like it, I suppose, but I once studied at old Brasenose. One of my class-mates became a bishop and sits in his lawn in the House of Lords, and another of them is a lord of the Admiralty and lives in Belgravia. Curse him! When I asked him to give me a berth in the dockyard, he had the impertinence to tell me that his duty to his country wouldn't allow him, and he turned me off with a guinea, the beggarly fellow, he did."

Lawrence said nothing, but he thought that very probably the Admiralty lord had good reasons for his conduct, and that he had been very generous as well.

"The more fool I. I've nobody to blame but myself for being here," went on the remorseful man. "But drink and dice and bad company would drag a bishop down to a beast—to say nothing of a reckless wretch like me. I have a brother who owns as fine an estate as any in Dorset. O! he's a highly respectable man"—this was uttered with a bitter ironical emphasis—"only drinks the very best port and sherry, while I had to put up with London gin or vile whisky. I couldn't abide his everlasting homilies, so I took ship to Quebec, and shook off the dust of my feet against them."

"Do your friends know you are in this country?" asked Lawrence, not seeing the relevancy of the quotation with which this speech closed.

"No, indeed, and I'll take good care that they shan't. They think I am dead. Best so ; and I *am* dead to them. No one would recognise in the seedy Matt Evans the fashionable man-about-town who used to lounge in the windows of the Pall Mall Club."

"Is that not your name?" asked, a little timidly, the innocent boy, who had slight knowledge of the wickedness and woe of the great world, and who looked with an infinite pity on this man so highly favoured with fortune and culture, almost as a sinless soul might look upon a ruined archangel, mighty though fallen.

"No, my boy, no one shall know that ; my secret shall die with me. But I rather like you. You are different from this herd around me here. Can I help you any in your Greek? I find I haven't forgotten it all yet."

Lawrence wondered to hear him speak thus of the men with whom he associated in all their coarse pleasures, and who, at least, had not fallen from the same height as he had ; but, hoping to interest him in some intellectual employment that might recall his better days, he said,

" I can't find the root of ἦλθον."

" O! that's irregular. Look for ἔρχομαι. That used to be quite a catch, that. Lots of these things in Greek. Did you ever hear of the bishop who devoted his whole life to verbs in μι, and on his death-bed wished he had confined himself exclusively to the middle voice ? Our old don at Brasenose wrote a big book on only the dative case. Those accents, too, are perplexing till you get the hang of them. If I had spent as much time learning English and common sense, as I have over the accents and Greek mythology, I should have been a wiser and a better man."

From this time he took quite an interest in Lawrence, and gave him a good deal of help in his difficulties with his Greek text. It was the first practical use, said this Oxford scholar, of which his Greek had ever been to him.

"WITH HIS LIGHT CANOE HE CAN GO ALMOST ANYWHERE."

CANOEING ON THE MATTAWA.

CHAPTER VII.

WAYSIDE SOWING.

" Sow in the morn thy seed,
  At eve hold not thy hand ,
To doubt and fear give thou no heed,
  Broad-cast it o'er the land.

Beside all waters sow ;
  The highway furrows stock ;
Drop it where thorns and thist es g ow ;
  Scatter it on the rock.

Thou know'st not which may thrive,
  The late or early sown ;
Grace keeps the precious germs alive,
  When and wherever strewn.

Thou canst not toil in vain :
  Cold, heat, and moist, and dry,
Shall foster and mature the grain
  For garners in the sky."
                        JAMES MONTGOMERY.

" SAY, Lawrence, have ye any other name ? " asked
  Dennis one day as he lay in his berth.

" Of course I have," said Lawrence. " Why do you
ask ? "

" Because I niver heared ye called anythin' else."
The shanty men do not often bestow on each other
more than one appellation.

" What is it, any way ? " he continued.

"Temple," was the reply.

"Timple! Timple Lawrence. Well, that's a quare name, now."

"No, Lawrence Temple," said his friend, smiling at the national propensity to put the cart before the horse.

"O! I thought Lawrence was the other name. And what for did they call you such an outlandish name as that?"

"I was born on the shores of the St. Lawrence. So they called me after the grand old river, and after a good old saint."

"Are ye named after a saint, and ye a Protestant? Well, now, isn't that quare? An' how did ye get your other name?"

"My father's name was Temple. How else would I get it?"

"Av course, I didn't think o' that," said the slow-witted Dennis. After a pause he went on. "Did ye iver know a praicher o' the name o' Timple?"

"My father was a preacher," said Lawrence, wondering if here was another link with that father's memory.

"Where did yer father praich?" asked Dennis.

"O! he preached all over—from the Ottawa to the Bay of Quinte," was the rather indefinite reply.

"Did he now?" exclaimed Dennis, in open-mouthed amazement. "Why, he must have been a bishop, or a canon, or some big gun or other in the Church. Wasn't he?"

"No," said Lawrence, "he was a plain Methodist minister."

"Why, the man I know'd was a Methodist too," continued the somewhat bewildered Irishman. "An' he used to praich at the Locks, near Kingston, ye know. There wuz a lot of men workin' at the canal—the Rideau canal, d'ye mind? And this praicher used to come there ivery two weeks. An' I worked wid

Squire Holton, an Englishman. Och, an' the good
farmer he wuz ! On'y to see the prathies and the oats
he raised. An' this praicher allus comed to his house,
d'ye mind ? An' I used to take care av his horse, for
he allus rode on horseback, exceptin' when he walked ;
an' then he didn't, av coorse. An' he was the dacint
gintleman, if he wor a Protestant. An' I mind he
allus comed to the stable, no matter how cowld or
wet he wuz—an' sometimes he wuz powerful wet,
ridin' through the bad roads,—an' the roads wuz bad,
shure enough, in the spring and fall.

"Well, as I wuz sayin', he allus comed to the
stable to see his horse rubbed down and fed—an' it's
himself knew how to curry a horse be-yutiful, for all he
wuz a rale gintleman. 'The marciful man is marciful
to his baste, Dennis,' he'd say. An' though he niver
gave me saxpince to drink his honour's health, though
it's meself often gave him the hint that it wouldn't
come amiss, yet many's the time he gave what's
betther : he gave me hapes o' good advice. 'Deed if
I had followed it I'd be a betther man the day. An'
one day, he says, says he, in his pleasant way, ye mind,
'Dinnis,' says he, 'my health's all right, an' the
best dhrink for yere health is jist cowld wather.' It
was his little joke, ye know.

"But I thought I'd be even wid him, an' I up and
towld him what Father O'Brady, the praste, said to
the tavern-kaper, that 'I just tuk a wee drap for my
stomach sake, like Timothy,' ye mind. But didn't he
get the joke on me ? 'Yere name's not Timothy,'
says he, 'an' there's nuthin' the matther wid yere
stomach, by the way ye made the prathies disappear
at dinner.' An' well he knew, for he sat right
forninst me at the table, ye see. More by token it
'ud be a long time in the ould coonthry afore I'd sit
down at the table wid a parson all in black—only he
wasn't in black but in butternut, but he had the
white choker any way : an' a rale clergyman he was,

too, as much as Father O'Brady or any o' thim, if he wuz a Protestant.

"When I was a poor dhrunken body, an' no man cared for my sowl, he talked to me like a father, he did, though he worn't as ould as meself. An' he tuk me one day into the hay mow—'twas jist as he was laving the sarcuit, as they called it—an' he made me knale down wid him on a truss o' hay. An' he knaled down beside me, an' he prayed for me—for me that niver prayed for meself, an' he cried over me, an' he made me promise to quit the dhrink. An' I did for a whole year, I did. Ohone! I wisht I had quit it for ever! I think I see him yet, wid the tears a-rinnin' down his cheeks, and him a-talkin' to the Almighty as if he saw Him face to face. Blessed Vargin! it's himself I see forninst me!"

The illusion was not unnatural, for Lawrence was very like his father. He had let Dennis run on in his garrulous way, knowing by experience that to interrupt him or to try to bring him to the point was like trying to guide an Irish pig to market by a cord fastened to its leg, only to make its wanderings still more erratic. He had listened with deep interest, and his sympathies were so aroused by the progress of the story that the tears stood in his eyes.

"It was my own dear father, Dennis," he said solemnly.

"Yere fayther!" exclaimed Dennis, the conviction of the fact bursting upon his mind like a flash. "An' so it was, blessin's on him, an' on ye too. I might have know'd it, ef it worn't for my born stupidity. Shure the saints haven't forgot me intirely to give me *two* such friends. They've got their hooks into me shure. An' to think that I trated the son of his riverence, Parson Timple, as I trated ye! I'm shure the divil must have *his* hooks into me, too, an a'tween 'em both I don't know which way they'll drag me, to heaven or hell. O wretched man that I am who shall save me from meself?" And he threw himself in a paroxysm of impassioned grief on his bed, unconscious that he had echoed the cry of the great Apostle of the Gentiles, which has been the cry of awakened souls, struggling with their heart of unbelief, through the ages, and shall be to the end of time.

Lawrence kindly pointed him to the only Refuge of sinners, trusting in Whom the Apostle Paul was able to change his cry of anguish into the doxology of joy, "I thank God, through Jesus Christ our Lord."

A few days after, Dennis said to his friend,

"What wuz the name of that Saint ye wor called afther, Mr. Lawrence, dear?"

"Why, Saint Lawrence, of course, who else should it be?" was the reply.

"Wuz it now? But av coorse it wuz, if I had only thought. Wuz he an Irish Saint, now?"

"No, he was a Roman. You never heard his story, I suppose?"

"No, nor his name, nayther."

"Well, he was one of the seven archdeacons of the Church at Rome when it was a pagan city, sixteen hundred years ago. The Christians were bitterly persecuted by a heathen Emperor whose name was Valerian. And Lawrence, who had charge of the property of the Church, its silver vessels and the like, thought it no harm to sell them to feed the poor starving, persecuted Christians."

"Nayther it was, I'm shure!" interjected Dennis.

"One day," continued the narrator of the ancient legend, "the Emperor sent a soldier to Lawrence to command him to give up the treasures of the Church. And he took the soldier to a room where were a lot of the old and sick and poor people whom he had rescued, and he said, 'These are the treasures of the Church.' And the soldier wouldn't believe but that he had gold hidden somewhere, and dragged him

4

before the Emperor, and he was cruelly scourged, and, they say, broiled to death upon a gridiron."

"Och! murther, now, wasn't that the cruel thing to do?" exclaimed the sympathetic listener; "and was *he* a Catholic?"

"He was a Catholic, as all good Christians are Catholics," said the namesake of the Saint, who would not relinquish to any section of the Church that grand old title of the Church Universal.

"But ye said he was a Roman," exclaimed Dennis, triumphantly, "so he must have been a Roman Catholic, and that is the best sort I'm thinkin'. Shure ye read me yerself the other night Saint Paul's 'pistle to Romans. Did he iver write one to the Methodists, now?"

Lawrence was compelled to admit that he had not; but he explained that the Methodist Church had only been in existence for about a hundred years.

"And how long since Paul wrote his 'pistle to the Romans?" asked Dennis eagerly, full of controversial zeal for the honour of his Church.

"Nearly eighteen hundred years," replied Lawrence.

"An' is the Catholic Church seventeen hundred years oulder than the Methodis'? Well, I'm thinkin' I'll jist wait till yours catches up to mine afore I'll jine it."

Lawrence, more anxious to have the man become a Christian than to have him become a Methodist, waived further argument, knowing that the breath of controversy often withers the tender flowers of religious feeling in the soul.

LOGGING IN THE LUMBER CAMP.

THE BURDEN BEARER.

INDIANS FISHING THROUGH THE ICE.

CHAPTER VIII.

THE LUMBER CAMP IN WINTER

" All night the snow came down, all night,
Silent and soft and silvery white ;
Gently robing in spotless folds
Town and tower and treeless wolds ;
On homes of the living, and graves of the dead,
Where each sleeper lies in his narrow bed ;
On the city's roofs, on the marts of trade,
On rustic hamlet and forest glade.

When the morn arose, all bright and fair,
A wondrous vision gleamed through the air ;
The world, transfigured and glorified,
Shone like the blessed and holy Bride—
The fair new earth, made free from sin,
All pure without and pure within,
Arrayed in robes of spotless white
For the Heavenly Bridegroom in glory dight."
WITHROW.

THAT beautiful season, the Canadian autumn,
passed rapidly by. The air was warm and
sunny and exhilarating by day, though cool by night.
The fringe of hardwood trees along the river's bank,
touched by the early frost as if by an enchanter's
wand, was changed to golden and scarlet and crimson,
of countless shades, and, in the transmitted sunlight,
gleamed with hues of vivid brilliancy. The forest

looked like Joseph in his coat of many colours, or like a mediæval herald, the vaunt-courier of the winter, with his tabard emblazoned with gules and gold.

Then the autumnal gusts careered like wild bandits through the woods, and wrestled with the gorgeous-foliaged trees, and despoiled them of their gold, and left them stripped naked and bare to shiver in the wintry blast. In their wild and prodigal glee they whirled the stolen gold in lavish largess through the air, and tossed it contemptuously aside to accumulate in drifts in the forest aisles, and in dark eddies by the river side. Then the gloomy sky lowered, and the sad rains wept, and the winds, as if stricken with remorse, wailed a requiem for the dead and perished flowers.

But there came a short season of reprieve before stern winter asserted his sway. A soft golden haze, like the aureole round the head of a saint in Tinto-retto's pictures, filled the air. The sun swung lower and lower in the sky, and viewed the earth with a pallid gleam. But the glory of the sunsets increased, and the delicate intricacy of the leafless trees was relieved against the glowing western sky, like a coral grove bathing its branches in a crimson sea.

Clouds of wild pigeons winged their way in wheel-ing squadrons through the air, at times almost darken-ing the sun. The wedge-shaped fleets of wild geese steered ever southward, and their strange wild clang fell from the clouds by night like the voice of spirits from the sky. The melancholy cry of the loons and solitary divers was heard, and long whirring flights of wild ducks rose from the water in the dim and misty dawn to continue their journey from the lonely nor-thern lakes and far-off shores of Hudson's Bay to the genial southern marshes and meres, piloted by that unerring Guide Who feedeth the young ravens when they cry, and giveth to the beasts of the earth their portion of meat in due season.

The squirrels had laid up their winter store of acorns and beech nuts, and could be seen whisking their bushy tails around the bare trunks of the trees. The partridges drummed in the woods, and the quail piped in the open glades. The profusion of feathered game gave quite a flavour of luxury to the meals of the shantymen, and was a temptation that few resisted to spend the hours of Sunday beating the woods or lurking on the shore for partridge or duck.

One morning, however, late in November, a strange stillness seemed to have fallen on the camp. Not a sound floated to the ear. A deep, muffled silence brooded over all things. When Lawrence rose and flung open the door of the shanty, the outer world seemed transfigured. The whole earth was clothed in robes of spotless white, " so as no fuller on earth can white them," like a bride adorned for her husband. Each twig and tree was wreathed with " ermine too dear for an earl." The stables and sheds were roofed as with marble of finest Carrara, carved into curving drifts with fine sharp ridges by the delicate chiseling of the wind. A spell seemed brooding over all,

> " Silence, silence everywhere—
> On the earth and on the air ; "

and out of the infinite bosom of the sky the feathery silence continued to float down.

But, alas ! earth's brightest beauty fades, its fairest loveliness is oftentimes defiled. Soon the trampling of teamsters, and horses, and lumber men besmirched and befouled the exquisite whiteness of the snow. But the untrodden forest aisles, and the broad ice-covered river, and the distant hills retained their virgin purity all winter long.

The lumbering operations were carried on with increased vigour during the winter season. War was waged with redoubled zeal upon the forest veterans, which, wrapping their dark secrets in their breasts,

and hoary with their covering of snow, looked venerable as Angelo's marble-limbed Hebrew seers.   When
beneath repeated blows of the axe, like giants stung
to death by gnats, they tottered and fell, the feathery
flakes flew high in air, and the huge trunks were half
buried in the drifts.   Then, sawn into logs or trimmed
into spars, they were dragged with much shouting
and commotion by the straining teams to the river
brink, or out on its frozen surface, as shown in the
engraving preceding Chapter IV., to be carried down by
the spring freshets towards their distant destination.

One night, when the snow lay deep upon the
ground and a biting frost made the logs of the shanty
crack with a report like a pistol shot, quite an
adventure occurred in the camp.   It was long after
midnight, and the weary lumbermen were in their
deepest sleep.   The fire had smouldered low upon
the hearth, and had become a bed of still burning
embers.   Suddenly there was heard a tremendous
commotion as of scratching and clawing on the roof,
then a heavy thud on the hearth as from some falling
body.   This was immediately followed by a deep
growl that startled out of sleep everybody not already
awake.   A smell of singed hair filled the shanty.   A
large black object was dimly seen in the faint light
rolling on the hearth, frantically scattering the red-
hot coals with its paws.   Presently the strange object
rolled off the elevated hearth and ran furiously round
the large room, and finally attempted to climb one
of the bunks.   The occupant of the latter, a profane
man, and a bully among his comrades, was at heart
an arrant coward—as bullies always are.   He thought
that his last hour had arrived, and that the arch-
enemy of mankind had come for his victim, and
roared lustily for help.   Lawrence, whose bunk was
near, although the fellow had been foremost in the
persecution of himself, ran to his assistance.

Leaning against the wall was a cant-hook, an

instrument much used by lumbermen for rolling
logs. It consists of a stout wooden lever, near the
end of which is attached by a swivel a strong curved
iron bar with a hook at its extremity. Seizing this,
Lawrence flung it over the bear's head, for bear it was,
and held him pinned to the ground by means of the
hook. His friend O'Neal now ran up with a gun
which he had hastily snatched from the rack above
his bunk. Placing the muzzle close to the bear's
head, he pulled the trigger, expecting to see the animal
roll over on the floor. The cap snapped, but no flash
followed.

"Och, murther," exclaimed Dennis, "it's not
loaded at all, shure! Didn't I draw the charge last
night, not expecting a visit from a bear before morning?"

Here Bruin, finding the constraint of his position
irksome, made a violent struggle and burst away from
Lawrence. He went careering round the shanty among
the half-dressed men, upsetting benches and tables,
snapping and snarling all the while, vigorously be-
laboured by the shantymen with clubs, crowbars, and
sled-stakes. At last he was driven to bay in a corner.
A gun was brought to bear upon him. He received
its discharge with a growl, and was soon despatched
with an axe.

It was found in the morning that, attracted probably
by the smell of the bacon that had been cooked for
supper, whose savoury odours still filled the shanty,
he had climbed on the roof by means of a "lean-to"
reaching near the ground. The crust of snow near
the central opening breaking under his weight, he was
precipitated, greatly to his own consternation, as well
as that of the inmates of the shanty, plump into the
middle of the hearth. His fat carcass made, however,
some amends for his unwelcome intrusion, and many
a laugh the shantymen enjoyed over the tender bear-
steaks as they recounted the adventures of the night.

To Lawrence, by universal assent, was awarded the skin, which proved a comfortable addition to his bed, as well as enabling him to fulfil the parting injunction of his brother Tom.

Poor Dennis did not soon hear the last of his exploit in shooting the bear with an empty gun, but he good-naturedly replied,

" Shure, who expected to see a baste like that come in the door through the roof without so much as ' By yer lave ? ' or even knockin' ? "

The pluck and coolness and daring exhibited by Lawrence on this occasion found him much favour in the eyes of the motley community of shantymen, as physical courage always will, even with those who had not appreciated the far nobler quality of his previous exhibitions of moral daring. They saw that the " gentleman," as they had resentfully called him, on account of his quiet personal dignity, was no milksop, at all events, and his boldness in the hour of confusion and danger was contrasted with the craven fear of the bully and pugilist of the camp.

" The Chevalier de la Tour," exclaimed Baptiste, " could not have been braver."

" He was quite a Cœur-de-Lion," chimed in Matt Evans.

" What's that? " asked one of the men.

" It means he haf de heart of a lion," said Baptiste.

" 'E got the 'eart of the bear any'ow," remarked a burly Yorkshireman, not seeing the force of the meta-phor, " and uncommon good heatin' it were."

During the cold weather the men no longer wandered in the woods on Sunday, but lounged around the camp, some firing at a mark, others snowballing or indulg-ing in rude horse play. Dennis O'Neal had com-pletely abandoned his Sabbath-breaking practices, and Lawrence read the Bible to him and some others whom he invited to join him. A few loungingly assented and

listened indifferently for a while, and then sauntered
away. It might be called a Bible class, only Lawrence
answered all the questions, and he had the only Bible
in the class. Dennis laboriously endeavoured to learn
to read the large type advertisements of an old copy of
the *Quebec Chronicle.* He said it was harder work
than chopping. And so it looked, to see him crouched
with contracted brow and pursed-up mouth over the
paper, following the letters with his clumsy fingers.

One Sunday he said to Lawrence, " Couldn't ye tip
us a bit of a sarmint, my boy ? Ye seem a chip o' the
ould block, an' ye ought to have praicher's timber in
ye, if ye're a son o' yer fayther."

Lawrence was somewhat startled at this suggestion,
but he modestly disavowed any ability to teach, much
less preach to, his fellow-labourers.

" Here we are all livin' like a lot o' haythens, and
sorra a bit o' difference betune Sunday and Monday,
except that the men smoke and swear and play cards
more. Shure can't ye talk to us all, as ye talked to me,
out o' the Good Book, d'ye mind, that time I was
hurted ? "

A great qualm came over Lawrence's soul at these
words. He promised to give an answer before night.
He then went out into the wintry woods to think and
pray over the matter. The spruces and pines stretched
out their snow-laden arms as if waving benedictions
upon him.*

> " Into the blithe and breathing air,
> Into the solemn wood,
> Solemn and silent everywhere !

---

* See this idea beautifully expressed in Longfellow's sonnet
on *The Benediction of the Trees.*

> ' Not only tongues of the apostles teach
>   Lessons of love and light, but these expanding
>   And sheltering boughs with all their leaves implore,
>   And say in language clear as human speech,
>   The peace of God that passeth understanding
>   Be and abide with you for ever more.' "

> Nature with folded hands seemed there
> Kneeling at her evening prayer,
> As one in prayer he stood."

He had endeavoured conscientiously to discharge every duty, and believed himself willing, as he had told his mother, if God and the Church called him, and Providence opened his way, to preach the Gospel. But he had thought that such a call must come in a regular way through the ordinary channel—through a vote of the quarterly meeting putting his name on the circuit plan as exhorter and local preacher.

But here, by the mouth of this illiterate Irishman, among rude men and far from Christian sympathy—could this be a call from God to bear this heavy cross? He knelt in the snow and prayed with such sense-absorbing earnestness that he did not feel the biting wind blowing on his bare forehead. He rose from his knees with the resolve that he would be willing to do God's will, whatever it might be, but still without the conviction that this was the will of God for him. The doubt was to be solved for him sooner than he thought.

ON THE UPPER OTTAWA.

SHOOTING A RAPID ON THE MATTAWA.

CHAPTER IX.

THE BEECH WOODS CAMP-MEETING.

"The groves were God's first temples. Ere man learned
To hew the shaft, and lay the architrave,
And spread the roof above them,—ere he framed
The lofty vault, to gather and roll back
The sound of anthems : in the darkling wood,
Amidst the cool and silence, he knelt down,
And offered to the Mightiest solemn thanks
And supplication."

BRYANT—*Forest Hymn.*

WHEN he reached the shanty Lawrence found that Dennis, with characteristic impulsiveness, had interpreted his promise in the sense that he himself had wished, and had announced that Lawrence would preach that night. The announcement was received with an amount of criticism which convinced the generous-hearted Irishman that few of the company shared his enthusiastic feelings on the subject. Matt Evans volunteered to read the Church service, on the ground of having been an Oxford scholar, who "might now have been in holy orders if he hadn't been rusticated from old Brasenose."

There were, however, two difficulties in the way. In the first place the audience did not seem to appreciate his offer, some of them, with a rude backwoods sense of the fitness of things, threatening, if he attempted such a mockery of religion, to give him an opportunity of preaching from a rail pulpit, meaning thereby that they would give him a gratuitous ride on that uncomfortable species of steed. The second difficulty was still harder to surmount: there was no Book of Common Prayer in the camp, and no one, not even this Oxford scholar, on whose education the resources of the great university of the Established Church, with its host of clerical professors and vast endowments. had been exhausted, knew more than fragmentary snatches of the order of prayer.

When Lawrence entered the shanty, therefore, he was met by Dennis with the startling information that he must preach to them, and that his congregation was all ready. Indeed, nearly half of the company present, most of them in the expectation of having some fun at the expense of the boy, as they called him, had gathered in one end of the large room and were lounging on benches or tables or reclining in the bunks. It was a rough-looking group—red-shirted almost to a man, bepatched, unshaven, and almost as shaggy and unkempt in appearance as the bear which had so unceremoniously entered the camp a few nights before. A couple of Indians stood in the background, silent and stoical, smoking their pipes. In other parts of the room were men playing cards, talking or smoking, one making an axe helve, another repairing a snow-shoe, and a third cleaning a gun.

Lawrence had never studied rhetoric, but he began with a good rhetorical stroke.

"Gentlemen," he said, "I never attempted to preach in my life, and I don't think I could if I tried ; but, if you wish it, I will be happy to read you a sermon a great deal better than any I could make."

The modesty of the lad pleased the fellows, but especially the complimentary title by which he addressed them. He had called them gentlemen, rough and ragged as they were, and they felt that they must not belie the character he had given them. There was, therefore, a murmur of applause, and he went to bring from his little kit his Bible, hymn-book, and an odd volume of Wesley's Works containing half-a-dozen of his sermons. He opened by accident at the hymn,—or was it accident? it seemed so strikingly appropriate to the soul-wants of his audience,—

> "O all that pass by, To Jesus draw near;
> He utters a cry, Ye sinners, give ear!
> From hell to retrieve you He spreads out His hands;
> Now, now to receive you He graciously stands.
>
> "If any man thirst And happy would be,
> The vilest and worst May come unto Me;
> May drink of My Spirit, Excepted is none,
> Lay claim to My merit, And take for his own."

The hymn was sung to a fervid lilting tune, and before it was finished everybody in the group was singing, and several from the other end of the room had joined the company.

Lawrence then said simply, "Let us pray," and, kneeling down, he fervently uttered the common needs of all human souls to the common Saviour of mankind. He seemed to forget where he was, and talked with God, not as to a Being afar off in the sky, but as to One near at hand, Who would hear and answer his petition.

Then they sang again, and Lawrence quietly read Mr. Wesley's grand sermon on Salvation by Faith. When he had got through, Evans, who during one of the intervals of singing had examined the book, said,

"It's all right, boys. That's sound doctrine. That old don was a clergyman of the Church of England, and a Fellow of Oxford University, and he must have been a pretty good scholar to have been that. See, here he is, gown and bands and all the rest of it," and he held up the historic portrait that has been familiar to successive generations of Methodists throughout the world.

"He mought ha' ben a great scholard," said Jim Dowler, a raw Canadian youth, "but he talks jist as plain as Parson Turner, the Methody preacher, up to our village, and *he* never wuz to no 'varsity 'xcept Backwoods College, as I knows on."

"What for is a man a scholard," asked Dennis O'Neal, very naturally, "unless to make hard things plain to unlarned folk?"

"Wal, I've seed college-larnt men that talked as if they'd swallered the dictionary an' it didn't agree with 'em—'twas so hard to get the hang o' their lingo," said our Canadian lad, who evidently had not acquired his vernacular from the dictionary.

"Did you know Mr. Turner?" asked Lawrence.

"Wal, yaas," said Dowler. "Ther wuzn't many folks in our parts as didn't know *him*. Mighty peart preacher, he wuz, I 'low. Had a great pertracted meeting up to Brian's Corners, and Jim Collins and Jack Scoresby, they fit to see which on 'em 'd go hum with Samantha Cummins, old widder Cummins' darter. An' 'tworn't three nights 'fore both on 'em got converted, they did, an' 'stead 'o fightin' 'bout Samantha Cummins they wouldn't nuther on 'em go with her 'cause she wore artificials and went to dancin' school. Did you know him?"

"Yes," said Lawrence, "he was on the Thornville Circuit last year."

"Blest if these Methodists ain't everywhere," said Evans.

"Wal, yaas," said Jim, "I've bin whar ye couldn't see no housen in five miles, 'way up the Otonabee River. Thar's whar I first seed Parson Turner: com'd all the way from the Bay o' Quinty, roads so bad couldn't ride, had to walk good part o' the way. I've know'd people walk five miles bar'foot to hear 'im preach, and bring their own candles, too; an' he never wuz to no college, nuther," he concluded triumphantly, as though he thought having been to college was in some respect a *dis*qualification for ministerial work.

" Let us 'ave some more de musique," said Baptiste, whose fine tenor voice was heard to advantage in the singing, "or I vill 'ave to gif vous de ' Roulant ma boule.' "

Lawrence now gave out in succession several of Charles Wesley's matchless lyrics, whose warmth of sentiment, vivid imagery, and hearty music strangely captivated the taste of these rude men. In this pleasant and profitable manner a portion of each Sunday and sometimes of a week evening was spent in the lumber camp.

As the stock of sermons in his precious volume became nearly exhausted Lawrence felt a good deal exercised in mind as to what he should do when he had gone through them all. This feeling was increased by the remark volunteered one Sunday by Dennis :

" That readin' 's all very well when ye can't get anythin' betther; but couldn't ye jist tip us a sarmint o' yer own, wunst in a while by way of a change ? "

" Yaas," said Dowler. "It don't seem to come hum to a feller like what it doos when ye speak it right outen your head, ye know. I see a college-larnt feller couldn't preach a sarmin no ways without his writin' afore 'im. Couldn't even say his prayers 'cept he read 'em outen a book. Guess he'd found it a hard sight preachin' at the camp-meeting at the Beech Woods, on the Otonabee Circuit. Old Elder Case wuz thar, his white hair a-streamin' in the wind while he exhorted the sinners—powerful hand to exhort, he wuz—an' a half-a-dozen prayin' at wunst, an' as many more shoutin' ' Halleluyer ! ' and ' Hosanner ! ' an' p'r'aps a dozen fellers laughin', mockin', an' crackin' their whips among the trees. Takes a pretty peart preacher to keep his head in a meetin' like that.

" But Elder Case, he kep' 'em well in hand. He'd

run a camp-meetin' jes as easy as I'd drive a yoke o'
breachy steers, an' I don't know but a great sight
easier. I see him wunst when Jim Crowther and
them fellers from Cavan, ' Cavan Blazers,' they used
to call 'em, an' pretty rough fellers they wuz, swore
they'd break up the camp-meetin'. Well, Jim Crowther,
he wuz the ringleader, an' he was a-cussin' an' a-
swearin', an' he says, ' Wait, boys, till I give the word,
an' then make a rush for the stand, an' we'll clar the
ranch o' 'em white-chokered fellers.' An' the old Elder,
he kep' his eye on 'em, an' he jes' kep' on a-prayin';
an' he ast the Lord to smite them that troubled Izrel,
and Jim Crowther, he began to tremble, an' soon he
fell right down, an' the Elder came an' prayed for 'im
an' talked with 'im, an', what d'ye think? that Jim
Crowther that used to bully the hull neighbourhood,
he got convarted, an' he used to pray an' sing hymns
as loud in meetin' as ever he swore an' sang songs at
the old Dog an' Gun tavern at Slocum's Corners."

"Oui, oui," said Baptiste La Tour, "ze preaching
all vere well, but me like ze muzique."

"Ye'd oughter heered the singin' at the Beech
Woods camp-meetin'," continued Dowler, to whom his
experience on that occasion had been one of the chief
events of his life. "When the meetin' got so noisy
he couldn't exhort no longer, then old Elder Case, he'd
sing, an' a powerful sweet singer he wuz, too. An'
ther wuz a band o' Christian Injuns used to come to the
meetin', an' it wus the touchin'est thing to hear those
poor creeters a-singin'—couldn't tell a word they said,
ye know; but the tunes wuz the same, an' their
voices wuz that sweet—well, I never heered nuthin'
like it.

"Mighty solemn the singin' wuz, too, sometimes;
made yer feel wuss nor the preachin'. I 'member one
night there'd ben a dreffle powerful sarmin by a tall,
dark man, Elder Metcalf wuz his name. P'r'aps
some on ye know'd 'im. It 'u'd e'en a-most make

yer hair stan' on end to listen to 'im. Then they sung
in a wailin' sort o' tune,—

> ' O, there'll be mournin', mournin', mournin', mournin',
> O, there'll be mournin' at the Jedgment-seat o' Christ ! '

" I never felt so bad as I did that night. I wanted
as much as could be to go forrad to the penitent
beuch ; but Bill Slocum he wouldn't, an' he made me
come away, an' the road through the woods wuz awful
dark, black as a wolf's jaws ; wuzn't no housen for two
miles, an' far behind us the bright lights wuz a-shinin'
in the trees ; it seemed like heaven a-most, an' we
seemed in the outer darkness, where there's a wailin'
an' gnashin' o' teeth, an' we could hear, a-sinkin'
an' a-swellin' in the distance, as the night wind blowed
an' moaned like evil sperits through the tops o' the
pines, them awful words o' that hymn,—

> " ' O, there'll be mournin' at the Jedgment-seat o' Christ ! '

" I niver wuz so skeart in all my born days. But
Bill Slocum, he coaxed me inter the tavern, an' he
drinked, an' he made me drink, an' I got drunk for the
first time in my life. It 'pears ever since then that
preachin' don't have no effect on me ; got past feelin',
kinder, I 'low. Many's the time I've wisht I'd gone to
the penitent bench that night. But now I'm afeared
it's too late, even if I had a chance ; " and the poor
boy heaved a deep and troubled sigh.

Lawrence tried to encourage the poor fellow with
the promises of Scripture, but nothing seemed to give
him so much comfort as singing the hymn,—

> " Come, ye sinners, poor and needy,
>   Weak and wounded, sick and sore ;
> Jesus ready stands to save you,
>   Full of pity, love, and power."

" That's one o' the hymns they used to sing at camp-
meetin'," said Dowler. " It 'ud be nice now ef I
could only b'lieve that 'ar. Wish to goodness I could,
but 'pears I can't b'lieve in nuthin' no more."

5

CHAPTER X.

FINDING THE FOLD.

" There were ninety and nine that safely lay
   In the shelter of the fold ;
And one was out on the hills away,
   Far off from the gates of gold ;
Away on the mountains wild and bare—
Away from the tender Shepherd's care.

' Lord, Thou hast here the ninety and nine—
   Are they not enough for Thee ? '
But the Shepherd made answer, ' This of Mine
   Has wandered away from Me ;
And, although the road be rough and steep,
I go to the desert to find My sheep.'

And all through the mountains thunder-riven,
   And up from the rocky steep,
There rose a cry to the gates of heaven,
   ' Rejoice, I have found My sheep ! '
And angels echoed around the throne.
' Rejoice, for the Lord brings back His own ! ' "

MISS CLEPHANE.

L AWRENCE took the poor lad outside of the lumber
shanty, and walking beneath the frosty stars he
talked to him out of his own experience—the surest
way of gaining access to a barred and bolted heart, and
of meeting the difficulties of a sincere and seeking
soul.   Still the cloud of darkness seemed to brood over
the mind of this poor raw lad, who was yet dimly conscious of the deep immortal need of his nature—the

hunger and thirst of his soul. Lawrence, about to
bid him good-night, shook him warmly by the hand
and promised to pray for him.

" Will yer now? that's very kind o' yer, what's such
a scholard to pray fur a poor, ign'rant feller like me ;
'pears to me it's time I wuz prayin' fur myself."

" Do," said Lawrence. " 'If any man lack wisdom,
let him ask of God.' He will guide and teach you
and bring you out all right, if you will only ask in
the name of Jesus and trust in Him."

" But I don't know no prayers," said the poor
fellow, " ain't said none since I wuz a little chap at
my mother's knee, long ago I kin remember."

" But you remember the Lord's Prayer, don't you? "
said Lawrence, in a sympathizing tone.

" I don't know," said the poor fellow ; " what is it
like ? "

Almost appalled at such deplorable ignorance in a
Christian land, Lawrence repeated that Litany of the
Ages in which are voiced the wants of God's great
family of suffering and sorrowing humanity.

" Seems to me I have heered that afore, at meetin',
or somewheres. But I ain't a boss hand at rememberin'.
It doos sound nice, though : ' Our Father '—that means
everybody's father, don't it? no matter how poor or
ign'rant or ragged, don't it ? Well, I ain't never had
no father 'cept to cuss and swear at mother and me,
and p'r'aps to beat us when he wuz drunk. I guess
God must be somethin' like what mother wuz. She
wuz amazin' good, I tell yer. I've know'd her, when
there wuzn't bread enough for Martha an' me, to stint
herself an' pretend to eat, and give it nearly all to us.
An' when father wuz bangin' things around, I've
know'd her to run between us an' him when he wuz
goin' to beat us,—jest like a hen kiverin' her chickens
when a hawk wuz arter them."

Happy he who rises to his highest conceptions of
the love of God from its sublimest earthly type—the

unwearying, utterly self-sacrificing love of a mother for her babes.

Deeply touched at the simple pathos of the poor lad's memories of his neglected childhood, Lawrence replied, "Yes, that's just like God. 'As one whom his mother comforteth, so will I comfort you,' He says ; and 'as a hen gathereth her chickens under her wings,' so Jesus said He would gather His human creatures, if they would only let Him."

"Did He, now? Why, I allers wuz afeard o' God, an' wanted to hide away from Him, ye know. Yet many's the time, when I've been a-huntin' in the woods, I've felt that lonely I didn't know what to do. An' it wuzn't company like Bill Slocum I wanted, but some one like mother, only stronger, some one that could help me keep away from the taverns. An' when I've seed the wood-pigeons in their nests *a-creuslin'* under the wings of the old bird, I jest wisht I could creep somewheres and be jest as safe an' as happy as they wuz. But then I'd go back to the tavern an' play cards with Bill Slocum, an' arterwards I'd feel wuss than ever."

"My brother," said Lawrence, solemnly, "God was calling you to Himself; His Spirit was striving with yours; He was saying, 'Son, give Me thy heart.'"

"An' 'stead o' listenin' to Him and obeyin' Him I listened to the devil, and minded him, and took to drink, although I know'd it killed my mother, and ruined my father. O, what an awful sinner I've been! D'ye think God 'ud forgive me after all?" asked this awakened soul with deep agitation of feeling, and with an eager, imploring look in his eyes.

"Yes, my brother, I am sure of it," replied Lawrence, with a quiet confidence that greatly reassured his faltering heart, bowed down beneath the weight of sins, now felt for the first time. "I am sure of it, for God, for Christ's sake, forgave me."

" But you never wuz such a sinner as I am," objected this despondent soul.

"Yes," said the minister's son, born and nurtured in the very lap of piety, "I never drank nor swore, it is true; but, with brighter light and clearer knowledge, I long resisted God, and was thus, I believe in my heart of hearts, a greater sinner in His sight than you. But no matter how great nor how many your sins may have been, still the love of God and the blood of Jesus Christ can outweigh them all."

" I think I understand what you mean," said Dowler. "I remember wunst when I wuz quite a little chap, mother left me to take care of Martha, while she went to milk the cows in the fur medder. An' she told me not to go into the woods for fear I'd get lost. An' when we wuz a-playin', I see such a purty butterfly, all purple and black and gold, an' I ran after it and Martha ran after me; an' when we came to the woods we saw such lots of flowers, the blue gentian and yellow golden rod, an' one splendid cardinal flower, they call it. An' we wandered on and on, and all at wunst we didn't know where we wuz at all. An' little Martha began to cry, an' I got so hungry, an' it got dark, an' we knew there wuz wolves in the woods, for we had often heerd them a-howlin' at night. But I felt wust of all 'cause mother'd come home an' find us gone, when she told us to stay.

"Well, Martha, she clean tuckered out, and couldn't go no furder, an' fell right down on the dried leaves. An' I sot down beside her, an' we waited there,—O, it seemed like all night!—an' Martha went asleep, but I wuz afear'd to shut my eyes for fear the wolves 'ud come and eat us. It wuz awful dark, I tell yer; and the wind wuz a-moanin' in the tops o' the pines so skeary-like. Bime-by I heard a shoutin' an' hollerin' in the woods, an' horns a-blowin', an' men a-beatin' the brush as if they wuz huntin' patridges.

"But I wouldn't leave little Martha for fear 1

couldn't find her again, an' when one of the men com'd
near I shouted as loud as I could, an' the man runn'd
to us with a great flarin' torch in his hand. An' who
should it be but father ! an' he hugged us and danced
and shouted—I never see him so glad in all my life.
An' he took Martha in his arms, and the men all com'd
where we wuz, an'we went home together. An' there
wuz mother on her knees a-reading of the Bible, an'
she jest jumped up and didn't say nothin', but hugged
us to her buzzum, the tears a-runnin' down her face
like rain. Father went off to the tavern to treat the
men ; an' nex' mornin' mother went into her bedroom
with Martha and me, an' knelt down an' thanked God
we'd been saved from the wolves. An' she asked me
if I didn't think I ought to be punished for takin'
little Martha into the woods ? And I said ' I know'd
I should.' An' she kissed me, an' cried, an' gave me
a good whippin', an' I never cried a bit, though it hurt
awful, 'cause I didn't want mother to feel any wuss
than she did. D'ye suppose I didn't know mother
loved me all the time, an' d'ye think I went to them
woods again ? No, sir-ree, an' it wuzn't the whippin'
kep' me, neither. I didn't want to make mother cry
again."

"It is just so with God," said Lawrence, who had
not interrupted this long reminiscence. "No mother
is so glad to rescue her child from death as He is to
welcome wandering sinners who return to Him. Though
He hates their sins, He loves their souls. And that
they might be saved, and at the same time their sins
not go unpunished, He gave His Son to suffer in our
room and stead, and Jesus bare our sins in His own
body on the cross."

"Yes, I heerd that afore, but I never seemed to
understand it, like. But those awful sins, that
drinkin', an' swearin', an' profanin' the name of that
Good Bein' that's been a-lovin' me all the time ; O,
how I hate them ! an' God bein' my helper, I won't

never do them again. But that won't make amends
for the past ! "

Patiently and lovingly Lawrence explained to this
untutored soul the way of salvation by faith in Jesus.
Retiring into the shadow of the trees, they knelt
down in the snow beneath the silent stars, and
wrestled with God in prayer. Lawrence used, as the
language of his petition for this struggling soul, that cry
of a penitent heart, the fifty-first Psalm, to every clause
of which the sin-convinced supplicant groaned assent.
As Lawrence uttered the verse, " Create in me a clean
heart, O God, and renew a right spirit within me," the
other sprang to his feet with the shout, " I've got it !
Halleluyer ! I've got it." As he afterward explained,
when able to express his feelings more calmly, while
he knelt with fast-closed eyes in the snow, his whole
soul concentrated in prayer, he seemed to behold, by
the eye of his mind, the Lord Jesus hanging bleeding,
interceding, on the cross. As He gazed, with a look
of infinite compassion in His eyes, He seemed to utter
in a tone of tenderest love, " Son, be of good cheer, thy
sins be forgiven thee," and instantly a tide of light
and peace and joy seemed to flood the earnest seeker's
soul. He grasped the hand of Lawrence and shook it
with vehemence, while tears of gladness flowed down
his cheeks.

His sympathizing friend gave vent to his feelings in
that grand exultant strain of Charles Wesley's :

> " My Jesus to know,
> And feel His blood flow,
> 'Tis life everlasting, 'tis heaven below.'

In this glad doxology the young convert joined, and
the long-drawn shadowy forest aisles rang with the
music of the strain, while angels in heaven struck
their harps in a more rapturous measure as they rejoiced over the conversion of a soul, the return to the

Father's house of a prodigal, long lost, now found again, once dead, but now alive.

As they twain walked together to the lumber-camp, all nature seemed transfigured. The silvery moonlight glistened on the snow like the glorified garments of the saints in heaven. The stars seemed to throb with sympathy and to burn with a tenderer and more lambent light. The snow-laden branches of the spruces seemed stretched in benediction over their heads, and the whisper of the night-wind among the pines seemed to breathe a blessing as it passed. Even the prosaic lumber shanty, with its squalid surroundings, seemed ennobled and dignified, and in some sense rendered awful, as being the arena in which immortal beings were working out their eternal destiny.

CAMPING OUT IN THE BACKWOODS.

MOOSE HUNTING IN CANADA.

CHAPTER XI.

THE MAIDEN SERMON.

"In doctrine uncorrupt, in language plain,
And plain in manner ; decent, solemn, chaste,
And natural in gesture ; much impressed
Himself, as conscious of his awful charge,
And anxious mainly that the flock he feeds
May feel it too ; affectionate in look,
And tender in address, as well becomes
A messenger of grace to guilty men."

COWPER—*The Task.*

LAWRENCE was greatly cheered and enbraved by this trophy of Divine grace vouchsafed to his humble efforts. He no longer therefore hesitated to take up the cross of trying to preach Christ to his fellow-men. On the following Sunday evening, accordingly, a tolerably numerous group were gathered in the shanty to hear his maiden sermon. Some were indifferent, some critical, and some sympathetic, for the lad was liked in the camp. His face had a rapt expression as he came in from his forest oratory, whither he had retired to seek strength from God in prayer.

He wished to talk to those hard-handed, toiling men, in such a manner as to enlist their interest and sympathy. He therefore selected as his text that Scripture in which the kingdom of heaven is likened to a householder who went into the market-place to hire labourers.   He gave out the exceedingly appropriate hymn—

> " Are there not in the labourer's day
>   Twelve hours, in which he safely may
>   His calling's work pursue ? "

He had the attention of his humble audience at
once.   And, what is more, he kept it to the end.   He
spoke to these, his fellow-workmen in his daily toils,
in a manly, simple, straightforward manner.   He
made no attempt at eloquence, an attempt that is
almost certain to defeat its object.   Like Mark
Antony, he only spoke right on what they themselves
did know, and completely carried with him the convictions of their judgment and the assent of their
wills ; and this, we take it, is the true object of the
highest kind of eloquence.

He spoke to them of life as the day of their work in
God's world, of His claims upon their love and labour,
of the grand opportunities and glorious reward He
offered them.   And as he gazed upon that company
of strong and stalwart, although uncouth and uncultivated men, he beheld not merely the rough red-shirted
lumber-men, but the candidates for an immortality of
weal or woe, who should in a few short years stand
with himself before the judgment seat of Christ to
receive the wage of their labour—the "Come, ye
blessed," that should welcome them to the joys of
heaven, or the "Depart, ye cursed," that should banish
them to the doom of the lost.   On this subject he
held strong, clear, intense convictions.   The thought
fired his soul.   It gave a burning vehemence to his
words, a pleading earnestness to his tones, a yearning
tenderness to his countenance, and made his eyes
glisten with unshed tears.   He spoke out of a full
heart and as a "dying man to dying men."

His rude auditors listened with more and more absorbed interest.   Presently one ceased to whittle the stick he held in his hand, another unconsciously let his pipe which he held in his mouth go out, another let the tobacco that he was cutting fall on the floor. Now sundry ejaculations of approval were heard, as, "That's so," "True for ye," "You bet," and still stronger expressions than these. But they caused no feeling of interruption or incongruity any more than the "Amen" or "Hallelujah" of a Methodist camp-meeting.

After an urgent appeal to accept the service and salvation of Christ, Lawrence gave out the hymn—

> "Ye thirsty for God, To Jesus give ear,
> And take, through His blood, A power to draw near;
> His kind invitation, Ye sinners, embrace,
> Accepting salvation, Salvation by grace."

He was fond of those long lilting tunes, which had a measured cadence in their swell like that of an ocean wave. The hymn was sung with a right good will, and after a fervent prayer Lawrence disappeared from their midst. He sought the dim recesses of the forest, and falling on his knees gave vent to his feelings in a gush of tears—tears of holy joy that he had been permitted to preach the glorious Message of the King, the Gospel of salvation to his fellow-men.

Every Sunday evening for the rest of the season was similarly employed. Even the most reckless voted that it was "better than playin' cards, an' didn't rile the temper so much either; though it did mak' 'em feel kinder bad sometimes, an' no mistake."

Jim Dowler, with the characteristic enthusiasm of a young convert, enjoyed these services immensely.

"That's the sort o' preachin' I like," he would say. "None o' yer readin' outen a book. Mr. Wesley's sermons may be all very good, but I like to look inter a man's eyes when he's a-talkin'; now this preachin' makes a body's soul feel good all the way down to his boots."

"Guess all the soul you've got's in your boots," sneered the Oxford scholar, who among other accomplishments had acquired at that great seat of learning an accent of scepticism and a tendency toward punning. "That kind of talk," he graciously admitted, "is not bad for a lumberman, and may do for the backwoods, but it would never do for old Brasenose."

"Who *is* ould Brasenose, any way?" inquired our friend Dennis O'Neal, who was greatly puzzled by Evans' frequent references to his *alma mater.* "Ould brazenhead he desarves to be called, if that prachin' wouldn't suit him."

CHAPTER XII.

CHRISTMAS AT THE LUMBER CAMP.

" Shepherds at the grange,
Where the Babe was born,
Sang with many a change
Christmas carols until morn.
Let us by the fire
Even higher
Sing them till the night expire.

Carol, carol, Christians,
Carol joyfully,—
Carol for the coming
Of Christ's Nativity ;
And pray a gladsome Christmas
For all good Christian men ;
Carol, carol, Christians,
For Christmas come again.
Carol, carol."

A SLIGHT break in the monotony of the winter was made by the festivities of Christmas and New Year. The French cook, Antoine La Croix, exhausted his professional skill in preparing a sumptuous dinner, and, truth to tell, the material elements of a substantial feast were not wanting. A pair of superb wild turkeys graced each end of the long table which was erected for the occasion. A haunch of venison had the place of honour in the middle. A ham of Lawrence's bear, which had been kept frozen in the snow, was boiled in the soup kettle. Beavers' tails procured from the Indians, wild ducks, a few of which still lingered, and wild pigeons also garnished the board. Dennis regretted, however, that the modicum of potatoes was so meagre, and Yorkshire John availed himself of his national privilege of grumbling at the absence of the "roast beef of hold Hengland." He was mollified, however, by the appearance of a plum-pudding of magnificent dimensions, which was turned out of the flour bag in which it was boiled into a huge wooden platter, deftly shaped with an axe for its reception. He found fresh cause of complaint, nevertheless, in the circumstance that the short allowance of "plums" was supplemented by a quantity of cranberries from the neighbouring marsh.

"What for do ye call them plums anyway when they're only raisins afther all?" queried Dennis. "Shure even a blunderin' Irishman like me knows betther nor that."

Out of deference to Lawrence, who had become recognised as a sort of domestic chaplain, he was requested by the "boss" of the shanty to say grace at this first meal to which the company had sat down together.

"Stop," exclaimed Evans, "I'll give you the Christmas chant they sing at Old Brasenose;" and he roared out the ancient stave :

> "The Boar's head in hand bear I,
> Bedecked with bays and rosemarye ;
> And I pray you, my masters, be merrie,
> *Quot estis in convivio,*
> *Caput apri defero,*
> *Reddens laudes Domino.*"

"Where's yere boar's head?" interrupted Dennis. "Whativer langwidge is that ye're spaking? It sounds like Father O'Brady sayin' mass, an' if it's the howly Roman tongue it's not fit for the likes o' ye to spake it. Come, Lawrence, darlint, don't let the praties be gettin' could, what there is of them. Sing us somethin' we all can understand."

Thus adjured, Lawrence gave out that metrical grace which has inaugurated so many Methodist festivals :

> "Be present at our table, Lord,
> Be here and everywhere adored ;
> These creatures bless, and grant that we
> May feast in paradise with Thee."

The valiant trenchermen then fell to work, and did ample justice to Antoine's cookery. His doughnuts and pudding elicited the heartiest commendation. Many a good-natured joke and jest and laugh went round the board—literally a board supported upon wooden trestles. Lawrence sat mostly silent, thinking of a little group of loved ones three hundred miles away that he knew were thinking of him as they sat down to their humble Christmas fare.

When dinner was over, Jean Baptiste, who always embraced an opportunity of exercising his skill, brought out his violin, and after sundry scrapings and tunings accompanied himself while he sang a French Christmas carol, or "Noel," as he called it, in the sweet, wild, beautiful refrain of which every one soon joined, even without knowing the meaning of the words.

Yorkshire John seemed to think the reputation of his country were gone if he could not cap the Frenchman's "outlandish ditty," as he called it, with an honest English stave.

"Ah !" he grumbled out with a sigh at the remembrance, "hold York's the place where they knaw hoo to ke-ap Christmas. Hoo the chimes 'ud ring oot oor the woald, an' the waissail bowl 'ud go roond, an' the waits 'ud sing ! Would ye loike to 'ear it?" and without waiting for an answer he rumbled out of his capacious chest the ancient carol :

"God rest you, merrie gentlemen
Let nothing you dismay,
For Jesus Christ, our Saviour,
Was born on Christmas Day,
To save us all from Satan's thrall,
Whose souls had gone astray.

Chorus.—God bless the master of this house,
God bless the mistress too,
And all the little children
That round the table go."

"Oi thinks Oi 'ears 'em noo," interrupted Long Tom of Lancashire. "Anoother one they used to sing in the West coontree was this;" and he trolled out the following:

"As Joseph was a-walking, he heard an angel sing,
'This night shall be born our Heavenly King;
He neither shall be born in housen nor in hall,
Nor in the place of Paradise, but in an ox's stall.

"'He neither shall be clothèd in purple nor in pall,
But in fair linen as were babies all;
He neither shall be rockèd in silver nor in gold
But in a wooden cradle, that rocks upon the mould.'"

"Yon moinds me," said Penryth Pengelly, a Cornish miner, who had been brought out to prospect for copper, a bootless task for him, "o' the toime when Oi wor a lad an' used to go a-Chris'masin', 'un' good yaale an' cakes we used to getten too, an' one o' the carols the fisher lads doon in oor parts—at St. Ives and yon ways—used to sing was this:

"I saw three ships come sailing in,
On Christmas D y, on Christmas Day,
I saw three ships come sailing in,
On Christmas Day in the morning.

"And what was in those ships all three,
On Christmas Day, on Christmas Day?
Our Saviour Christ and His Ladie,
On Christmas Day in the morning.

"And all the bells on earth shall ring,
On Christmas Day, on Christmas Day,

And all the angels in heaven shall sing
On Christmas Day in the morning."

"We didn't have thim haythin carolin's in ould Wicklow," said Dennis. "But we wint to chapel at midnight loike dacint Christians, an' moighty purty it luked, I tell yees, to see the altar all pranked wid flowers, an' the stall, an' the oxen, an' the Howly Vargin, an' the Blessed Babe an' St. Joseph, all as nat'rel as life. An' it's mesilf was one of the altar boys, no less, that used to help Father O'Shaughnessy. An' I 'member he had moighty hard work to tache me the office for Christmas Eve. What's this it was now?" he continued, scratching his head, screwing up his mouth, and squinting with one eye at the roof. "'Dade an' it's all clane gone but this bit :

"'Adeste fideles, læti, triumphantes,
Venite, venite, in Bethlehem.'

Though what 'twas all about I know'd no more than the Blessed Babe in the manger.

"They tell a cur'us thing in thim parts. I niver saw it mesilf, though I often watched, but Father O'Shaughnessy, he was the parish praste of Inniskerry, d'ye moind, he said it was so ; an' so it had to be so even if it wuzzen't so. I'd belave his word against my own eyesight, any day. D'ye think I'd be settin' my eyes against the praste's tongue that talks Latin loike a book? Not I, indade! I've larned my manners betther."

"What is it, any way?" "Out with it, man," "What's your story?" interrupted several of his impatient auditors.

"Well, his riverince declar'd," said Dennis solemnly, "that when he went to the stable to get his pony late on Christmas Eve to come to the sarvice, that the baste was down on his knees and the cows and the donkey all a-payin' obaysince to the Blessed Babe in the manger at Bethlehem."

"I suppose they were asleep," remarked the sceptical Matt Evans.

"Slapin', is it ye say, ye unbelavin' heretic?" retorted Dennis, who had not yet shaken off his native superstition, with a most contemptuous sneer at the bare suggestion. "P'raps ye'd say the praste was slapin' whin he saw on the flure all around his lanthern a bright light just like the glory round the head o' the Vargin?"

"Shouldn't wonder," said Evans, giving a rationalistic explanation of the phenomenon. "Does not the immortal William say that then

'The bird of dawning singeth all night long,
No fairy takes, nor witch hath power to charm,
So hallowed and so gracious is the time'?"

"Is it William of Orange he manes?" asked Dennis in a loud whisper as he nudged Lawrence. "It's him these Cavan fellows call Immortial."

Evans proposed to give, in contrast to the vulgar folk-songs to which they had been listening, the classic legend of "Good King Wenceslas" as they used to sing it at Brasenose. To his surprise, however, it fell as flat as the chant of the "Boar's Head."

"When I lived up to Kingston," here remarked Jim Dowler, who had hitherto kept silence, "I went a few Sundays to the Methodis' Sunday school there. I wuz a canal boy ridin' a hoss on the towpath then, and oftens I wuz that tired I went asleep on the hoss's back. Well, one Chris'mas time the teacher larned us some verses. 'Twas the only thing I *could* larn. 'Stonishin' how these things do stick to yer—wuss nor burdocks in a hoss's mane. Can't get rid on 'em no ways. I ain't much of a jidge o' po'try, but I thought they wuz rale purty then, when I didn't know their hull meanin'; an' now that I doos, I think they're partier still." And he sang the sweet old hymn:

"Hark! the herald angels sing
Glory to the new-born King,

'Peace on earth, and mercy mild ;
God and sinners reconciled.' "

Lawrence took advantage of the opportunity to say a few kindly and seasonable words about God's great Christmas gift to man, and the duty of living to His glory and in good-will to one another.

After dinner there were out-of-door games—la crosse, which they learned from a band of Indians camping near ; snow-shoeing, the trips and falls accompanying which occasioned much merriment ; snow-balling, shooting at a mark, and the like. The day passed very pleasantly, and, as a result of the absence of intoxicating liquor from the camp, without any of those degrading scenes of drunkenness which too often convert a Christian festival into the semblance of a heathen bacchanalian orgy.

New Year's Day had no very special celebration. On New Year's Eve, however, Lawrence held a sort of watch-night prayer meeting with a number of the more seriously inclined shantymen. The more boisterous members of the camp went out of doors to welcome the New Year with cheers and the firing of guns. Those that remained were more impressed by the solemn silence in which the death of the Old and advent of the New Year were awaited than even by the spoken prayers. It seemed as though the trickling of the golden sands of time was heard amid the hush, as God's hand turned the great glass of eternity in which the years are but as hours and the days as moments.

CHAPTER XIII.

AN ADVENTURE WITH WOLVES.

"Fearfully fares
The Fenris-wolf
Over the fields of men,
When he is loosed."
THE YOUNGER EDDA—*The Lay of Hazkon.*

THE remainder of the winter passed rapidly away in the daily routine of labour. In the month of March, when the snow lay deep upon the ground, Lawrence was despatched by the "boss" lumberman to Ottawa, a distance of some two hundred miles, to report to the agent of the Company the quantity of timber that had been got out, and to bring back from the bank a sum of money to pay off a number of the lumbermen. Several of these were about to take up land in the new townships which had been recently laid out on the Upper Ottawa, and as Lawrence had won the confidence of the Company, he was commissioned to bring back the money required for making the payments. Owing to a prejudice on the part of the men against paper money, he was directed to procure gold and silver. He was to ride as far as the town of Pembroke, about half way, and, leaving his horse there to rest, was to go on to Ottawa in the stage.

DOG TRAIN AND INDIAN RUNNER.

He selected for the journey the best animal in the
stable—a tall, gaunt, sinewy mare, of rather ungainly
figure, but with an immense amount of *go* in her.

He reached Ottawa safely, posted to his mother and
sisters a bulky epistle on which he had spent several
evenings, and transacted his business satisfactorily.
A couple of evenings were spent very pleasantly with
his friend, Mr. Daily, who was overjoyed to hear of his
welfare.

"I knowed that blood would tell," that person
asseverated, "and that the son of John Temple would
come out all right."

Having drawn the money from the bank, chiefly in
English sovereigns and Mexican dollars, Lawrence set
out on his return journey. At Pembroke he mounted
again his faithful steed for his ride of over a hundred
miles to the camp. The silver he carried in two
leathern bags in the holsters of the saddle, and the
gold in a belt around his waist. He also carried for
defence one of the newly-invented Colt's revolvers.

The weather was bitterly cold, but the exercise of
riding kept him quite warm. The entire winter had
been one of unprecedented severity. The snow fell
early and deep, and remained all through the season.
Deer were exceedingly numerous, even near the settlements ; and at the camp furnished no inconsiderable
portion of the food of the men, varied by an occasional
relish of bear's meat.

Toward the close of the second day he was approaching the end of his journey, and indulging in a pleasant
anticipation of the feast of venison he should enjoy,
and of the refreshing slumber on the fragrant pine-
boughs, earned by continued exercise in the open air.
The moon was near the full, but partially obscured by
light and fleecy clouds.

He was approaching a slight clearing when he
observed two long lithe animals spring out of the
woods towards his horse. He thought they were a

couple of those large shaggy deerhounds which are sometimes employed near the lumber camps for hunting cariboo,—great powerful animals with immense length of limb and depth of chest,—and looked around for the appearance of the hunter, who, he thought, could not be far off. He was surprised, however, not to hear the deep-mouthed bay characteristic of these hounds, but instead a guttural snarl which, nevertheless, appeared to affect the mare in a most unaccountable manner. A shiver seemed to convulse her frame, and shaking herself together she started off on a long swinging trot, which soon broke into a gallop that got over the ground amazingly fast.

But her best speed could not outstrip that of the creatures which bounded in long leaps by her side, occasionally springing at her hams, their white teeth glistening in the moonlight, and snapping when they closed like a steel-trap. When he caught the first glimpse of the fiery flashing of their eyes, there came the blood-curdling revelation that these were no hounds, but hungry wolves, that bore him such sinister company. All the dread hunters' tales of lone trappers lost in the woods, and their gnawed bones discovered in the spring beside their steel-traps, flashed through his mind like a thought of horror.

His only safety he knew was in the speed of his mare, and she was handicapped in this race for life with about five-and-twenty pounds of silver in each holster. Seeing that she was evidently flagging under this tremendous pace, he resolved to abandon the money. "Skin for skin, yea, all that a man hath will he give for his life;" so he dropped both bags on the road. To his surprise the animals stopped as if they had been highwaymen seeking only his money and not his life. He could hear them snarling over the stout leather bags, but, lightened of her load, the mare sprang forward in a splendid hand gallop that covered the ground in gallant style.

He was beginning to hope that he had fairly distanced the brutes, when their horrid yelp and melancholy long-drawn howl grew stronger on the wind, and soon they were again abreast of the mare.

He now threw down his thick leather gauntlets with the hope of delaying them, but it only caused a detention of a few minutes while they greedily devoured them. He was rapidly nearing the camp ; if he could keep them at bay for twenty or thirty minutes more, he. would be safe. As a last resort he drew his revolver, scarce hoping in his headlong pace to hit the bounding, leaping objects by his side. Moreover, they had both hitherto kept on the left side of the mare, which lessened his chance as a marksman. The mare, too, who was exceedingly nervous, could never stand fire ; and if he should miss and in the movement be dismounted, he knew that in five minutes the maw of those ravenous beasts would be his grave.

One of the brutes now made a spring for the mare's throat, but, failing to grasp it, fell on the right side of the animal. Gathering himself up, he bounded in front of her, and made a dash at the rider, catching and clinging to the mare's right shoulder. The white foam fell from his mouth and flecked his dark and shaggy breast. Lawrence could feel his hot breath on his naked hand. The fiendish glare of those eyes he never in all his life forgot. It haunted him for years in midnight slumbers, from which he awoke trembling and bathed in the cold perspiration of terror. He could easily have believed the weird stories of lycanthropy, in which Satanic agency was feigned to have changed men for their crimes into were-wolves— ravenous creatures who added human or fiendish passion and malignancy of hate to the bestial appetite for human flesh. If ever there was murder in a glance, it was in that of those demon-eyes that glared into those of Lawrence, and which seemed actually to blaze with a baleful greenish light—a flame of inextinguishable rage.

Lawrence felt that the supreme moment had come. One or other of them must die. In five minutes more he would be safe in the camp, or else be a mangled corpse. He lifted up his heart in prayer to God, and then felt strangely calm and collected. The muzzle of his revolver almost touched the brute's nose. He pulled the trigger. A flash, a crash, the green eyes blazed with tenfold fury, the huge form fell heavily to the ground, and in the same moment the mare reared almost upright, nearly unseating her rider and shaking his pistol from his hand, and then plunging forward rapidly covered the road in her flight.

As Lawrence had expected, the other famishing beast remained to devour its fellow. He galloped into the camp, almost fell from his mare, which stood with a look of human gladness in her eyes, and staggered to the rude log shanty, where the blazing fire and song and story beguiled the winter night, scarce able to narrate his peril and escape. After light refreshment, for he had lost all relish for food, he went to bed, to start up often through the night under the glare of those terrible eyes, and to renew the horror he had undergone.

In the morning, returning with a number of the men to look for the money, he found the feet, tail, muzzle, and scalp of the slain wolf in the midst of a patch of gory snow, also the skull and part of the larger bones, but gnawed and split in order to get at the marrow. And such, thought Lawrence, would have been his fate but for the merciful Providence by which he was preserved. They found also, some distance back, the straps and buckles of the money bag, and the silver coins scattered on the ground and partially covered by the snow.

WEST WIND'S INDIAN CAMP.

WEST WIND IN WAR PAINT.

CHAPTER XIV.

" Then the Black-Robe chief, the prophet
Told his message to the people,
Told the purport of his mission,
Told them of the Virgin Mary,
And her blessed Son, the Saviour ;
How in distant lands and ages
He had lived on earth as we do ;
How He fasted, prayed, and laboured;
How the Jews, the tribe accursèd,
Mocked Him, scourged Him, crucified Him ;
How He rose from where they laid Him
Walked again with His disciples,
And ascended into heaven."
LONGFELLOW—*Hiawatha.*

TOWARDS the close of the winter, when the length-
ened days and warmer radiance of the sun caused
the sap to stir beneath the bark of the trees, like
the returning pulse of life in a body restored from
suspended animation, a band of Indians pitched their
camp in a belt of sugar maples that grew alongside the
banks of the Mattawa.   They soon stripped great sheets
of bark from the white-skinned birches, leaving the gap-
ing wounds bleeding and raw, like some half-flayed creatures of the woods.   Birchen vessels were soon sewn
together by the deft fingers of the squaws.   Deep in-
cisions were made in the trunks of the maples with
a hatchet, and the escaping sap was collected in the

troughs. The kettles were swung, and the process of sugar-making was soon in full operation.

Lawrence found his way together with Jim Dowler to the camp one Sunday afternoon, impelled by an ardent desire to tell these poor wanderers of the woods of a fairer land than the fabled hunting-grounds of their fathers in the spirit-world—of the great All-Father of the red and the white alike, the true Great Spirit who will have men to worship Him in spirit and in truth. They expected to find the Indians engaged at their usual work—boiling sugar, making snow-shoes, and the like—taking no note of the Christian Sabbath. To their surprise they found everything quiet in the camp, the only exception being two little Indian lads with their dog digging out a badger from under the root of an old hemlock.

They approached the largest wigwam, a conical structure of birch bark stretched over tent poles, and drew aside the blanket that covered the opening which served as a door. A fire smouldered in the midst, its pungent smoke slowly escaping out of the opening at the peak of the wigwam. Crouched or squatted on mats or on bear or deer skins, were a number of Indians and squaws, young and old, with some children.

Through the smoke, at the further side of the wigwam, Lawrence saw the chief, a venerable old man with strongly marked features which looked as if carved in mahogany or cast in bronze. His iron-grey hair was bound by a wampum fillet about his brow. He wore a blanket coat, deer-skin leggings, fringed with beads, and moccasins. On his breast was a silver medal which Lawrence had never seen before. Most of the squaws sat with their bright-coloured shawls drawn over their heads, and wore gilt or glass beads around their necks. A tame raven hopped about and eyed the intruders with a grave and somewhat supercilious air. He gave a loud croak, as if to call attention to their presence, of which no one had yet taken any notice. An Indian near the door made room for them beside him, and motioned to them to sit down. They did so in silence, wondering what this strange conclave meant.

The old chief had on his knees a large leather-bound book—the last thing Lawrence expected to find in an Indian wigwam—and was apparently reading from its pages. In a deep, guttural, yet not unmusical tone he went on, his voice rising and falling like the voice of the wind among the pines. Once or twice Lawrence thought he caught the words "*Gitche Manitou,*" the Indian name for the Great Spirit or God, but he was not sure. At length, to his surprise and delight he recognised the familiar names "Jesus," and "Mary," and "Martha," and "Lazarus." This, then, was an Indian translation of the New Testament, of the existence of which Lawrence had never dreamed, and this must be a band of Christian Indians, and the venerable chief was reading the touching story of the resurrection of Lazarus.

When he had done reading, the old man looked significantly at one of the younger squaws, who thereupon began to sing a sweet, low, plaintive strain, in which she was joined by all present.

Lawrence did not, of course, understand the words, but the tune was the familiar "Old Hundred."

"That's the Doxology," said Dowler, who had often heard it at camp-meeting, and they joined, in English, in singing that anthem of praise which ascends to the God and Father of us all from every land and in almost every tongue.

The old man then rose, and kneeling reverently, as did all the company, prayed devoutly, concluding with an earnest "Amen," in which his white visitors heartily joined.

When they rose, the chief with a frank smile gave his guests the usual salutation, "Bo' jou'," a corrup-

tion of the French "Bon jour," which has passed into
the Indian language—a striking illustration, as are
the French names of lake and river all over the
continent, of the widespread influence of those intrepid
explorers and pioneers. Kewaydin or West-wind,
such was the chief's name, made room for Lawrence
and Dowler on the rug beside him, and courteously
offered them a curiously carved pipe of tobacco with
a red stone bowl and ornamented with brilliantly
dyed heron's and woodpecker's feathers. Lawrence
politely declined the honour, having, from respect to
his father's example and his mother's well-understood
wishes, never learned to use the vile weed. Dowler,
however, accepted it, and was soon vigorously puffing
away.

Lawrence picked up the Bible, which bore, he saw,
the imprint of that noble institution, the British and
Foreign Bible Society, whose various versions of the
Word of God are found alike in the Indian wigwam,
the Kaffir's kraal, the Hindoo bazaar or bungalow,
the Tartar's wandering tent, and the Esquimaux stone
cabin, and which speaks to the tribes of men the
unsearchable wisdom of God in almost all of the
babbling tongues of earth.

"Where did you get this?" asked Lawrence in
wondering tones.

"That," said the old man, who spoke English with
tolerable facility, "was the parting gift of the best
friend that Kewaydin, and many another poor Injun,
ever had—good old Elder Case—God bless him!"

"Did you know Elder Case?" exclaimed Dowler.
"I've heared him at the Beechwoods Camp-meetin'."

"When I forget him I'll forget to breathe," said
the old man fervently. "I owe him everything. He
found me a poor miserable pagan, a-drinkin' fire-
water, and beatin' the conjurer's drum and sacrificin'
the white dog, and he made me what I am."

Lawrence was overjoyed to meet this unexpected result of Methodist labour in an Indian wigwam. They talked together long and lovingly of the zealous apostle to the Indian tribes of Canada, and Lawrence ventured on a few practical reflections on the story of the raising of Lazarus, which had been the subject of the reading, and on the glorious inspirations it imparted. These were translated by the chief, and the company manifested their approval by sundry ejaculations and comments in their own language.

"Whar did ye git this?" inquired Dowler, laying his finger on the silver medal that decorated the chief's broad breast.

"That," said the old man, his eagle eye flashing proudly, "was fastened on my breast in full parade before all the red-coats by Major-General Sir Isaac Brock. See, that is King George's head. I always wear it on Sundays. It 'minds me of old times."

"Tell us all about it," said Dowler eagerly. "My father fit with Brock at Queenston Heights, an' arterwards got wounded at Lundy's Lane."

"Did he?" said the chief. "Well, I don't talk much of these things, but I don't mind telling the son of an old soldier. I entered Fort Detroit side by side with General Brock. It was for that I got the medal. Nine weeks after, I saw him fall at the Big Rapids (Queenston Heights). I helped to carry his body down the hill to the old house, where it lay—that great warrior just like Indian's dead papoose. I stood beside his grave and helped to fire the last volley over his body. But I helped to avenge his death, as we drove the 'Merican blue-coats over the cliff," with sudden energy exclaimed the veteran brave.

But with a tone of compunction he continued, "God forgive me, it was in my pagan days, when I seemed to thirst for blood. It was dreadful to see blue-coats

and red-coats struggling together like catamounts, and
to see the 'Merican militia rolling down the rocks, torn
by the jagged spruces, and some of them struggling in
the boiling eddies of the river.   One man was just
going to shoot a British captain when I flung my toma-
hawk right in his face.   He went crashing over the
bank, clutching at the spruce boughs, an' he looked
right into my eyes with such a dying agony—it's thirty
years ago, but I often see it still when I close my eyes
at night, and sometimes even when I try to pray.   I
used to gloat on it in my heathen days, but ever since
Elder Case taught me of the Blessed Lord who prayed
for His murderers and said, ' Love your enemies,' I
have wished I could ask that man's forgiveness before
I meet him at the last great review day when all the
soldiers and braves—English, 'Mericans, and Injuns—
must stand before the great Captain, the Lord Jesus.
He may have had little papooses and a white squaw
who wept for him·just as mine would weep for me.
But, thank God, I saved other lives that day.   My
braves were mad with slaughter, just as if they were
drunk with fire-water ; but when the victory was fairly
won I dragged them off the prisoners they were going
to scalp, though it was like tearing an eagle from a
heron he has struck, or the dogs off the haunches of
a deer.   This killing seems to come natural to the
pagan Injun of the woods, but for white men and
Christians it seems strange work."

"Yet ther' wuz Chris'n men that fit thar," interrupted Dowler.   "I hear'd father tell on a Methodis'
preacher—a local, ye know, not a reg'lar—who used
to preach an' pray an' sing like thunder in bar-
racks ; an' he fit like a tiger when the guns was a-
rattlin', an' kep' on praying all the time.   Yet he wuz
gentle as a lamb arter the fight, and used to nuss
the wounded—even the 'Merikers, too, jist as lovin'
an' tender as a woman."

In answer to the inquiry of Lawrence if the Christian

converts among the Indians received much opposition from their pagan relatives, the old chief told the following story :

"Did you notice that girl with the great scar on her forehead that sat yonder?" pointing to near the door, where had sat an Indian maiden lithe and graceful as one of the mountain birches, with eyes as deep and dark as a forest lake. "Well, she's Big Bear's daughter. He had a streak o' luck winter before last and had two big moose to spare. So he hitched up the dogs and drove down the river on the ice with them and some otter and mink furs to Oka, where the priests have a seminary and a convent. Mère Marie at the convent was buying some mink skins, and asked him if he wouldn't let his pretty daughter, Red Fawn, come and work in the kitchen, and she'd teach her to cook and sew. He wanted to please the nuns, so he let her go.

"Well, the nuns taught her to say the *Ave* and *Credo* and to dress the altar of the Virgin. I know their ways, I've lived among the Catholics. Very loving the nuns are when they like, and the poor girl never had any kindness showed her before. So they taught her the catechism, then the priest wanted her to be baptized. They get lots of Injun girls that way, mighty cunning them priests are, beat even an Injun for that. And they called her Marguerite des Anges, which means in the French language 'Pearl of the Angels.' And they gave her a pretty gilt crucifix to wear on her neck.

"Well, next fall Big Bear was camping down the river, and he went to see Marguerite. He met her in the woods gathering the late autumn flowers to dress the altar. She'd grow'd so tall an' handsome he was quite proud of her.

"'Come back, Ahduk, an' share my lodge,' he said; but she said she couldn't leave the kind good nuns.

"'You *must* leave these Christian dogs,' he shouted,
'or the wily Black-robes will make you a woman
worshipper like themselves.'

"'Nay, father, I like not the wild hunter's life,'
said Marguerite, and crossing herself, she went on: 'I
have already vowed to live the handmaid of Christ and
His blessed Mother, whom, O father! I beseech you
blaspheme not.'

"What! a daughter of mine become a sister of those
pale-faced nuns!' he cried. 'Why did I leave you
among them? I might have known they would teach
you to despise the gods of your father.'

"'But those be no gods, father,' she replied, 'but
evil spirits, says the priest, beguiling the souls of men
to perdition.'

"'Good enough gods for your old father,' he passionately answered, 'and good enough they must be for
his stubborn child. Know, girl, I have promised that
when the next snow comes, you shall keep the lodge-
fire of Black Snake, the bravest warrior of our tribe.'

"'Nay, father,' exclaimed the girl with a shudder,
'that can never be : I shrink when I see his glittering
eye and gliding step, as though he were indeed a
poisonous snake.'

"'It shall be, girl,' he thundered. 'Big Bear has
said it, and the word of Big Bear was never broken.'

"'Father, it cannot be,' said the brave girl ; 'I
will die first ; ' and in her firm-pressed lips and flashing
eye Big Bear saw that she had all his own determination
in her slender frame.

"'Then die you shall if you obey not my command,'
he hissed. Snatching the cross from her neck, he
stamped it beneath his feet, exclaiming, 'The accursed
medicine-charm, you love it, do you? then you shall
wear it in your flesh ;' and seizing his scalping knife he
gashed the sign of the cross upon her forehead, and
dragged her off bleeding and fainting to his wigwam.

"A few weeks after, before the wound was well

healed, when he wanted to give her to that scoundrel, Black Snake, she fled through the wintry snow to our camp and besought my protection, and my protection she shall have as if she were my own daughter—*they* are all dead now—so long as this gun can shoot game in the woods," he ended, pointing to his trusty fowling-piece.

"Is she still a Catholic?" asked Lawrence, who had been a deeply interested listener to this tragic recital.

"She has mostly forgotten the *Aves* and *Paters* that she didn't understand," replied Kewaydin, "but, instead, she sings in our own tongue the sweet hymns,

'When I survey the wondrous cross,'

'There is a fountain filled with blood,'

and many others. And one day when I was reading in the Good Book the words of Paul, 'I bear in my body the marks of the Lord Jesus,' she smiled and laid her finger on the cross-shaped scar on her forehead, and said, 'I, too, bear His sign in my flesh.' And she is so good and gentle and patient I sometimes think she is like the saints spoken of in the Revelation, who have come out of great tribulation, and have been sealed with the seal of God in their foreheads."

7

CHAPTER XV.

THE "TIMBER JAM."

"Now suddenly the waters boil and leap,
 On either side the foamy spray is cast,
Hoarse Genii through the shouting rapid sweep,
And pilot us unharmed adown the hissing steep,
 Again the troubled deep heaps surge on surge,
 And howling billows sweep the waters dark,
Stunning the ear with their stentorian dirge,
That loudens as they strike the rock's resisting verge.
        SANGSTER—*The St. Lawrence and the Saguenay.*

AT last the spring came to the lumber-camp. The days grew long and bright and warm. The ice on the river became sodden and water-logged, or broke up into great cakes beneath the rising water. The snow on the upland rapidly melted away, and the utmost energy was employed in getting down the logs to the river before it entirely disappeared. The harsh voice of the blue jay was heard screaming in the forest, and its bright form was seen flitting about in the sunlight. The blithe note of the robin rang through the air. A green flush crept over the trees, and then suddenly they burgeoned out into tender leafage. The catkins of the birch and maple showered down upon the ground. A warm south wind blew, bringing on its wings a copious rain. The river rose several feet in a single

night. One timber boom above the camp broke with
the strain upon it, and thousands of logs went racing
and rushing, like maddened herds of sea-horses, down
the stream. Happily the heavy boom below held firm,
and they were all retained.

About a mile above the camp was a steep and heavy
rapid of many rods in length. Above it a large
"drive" of logs had been collected. It was a grand
and exciting sight to see them shooting the rapids
As they glided out of the placid water above, they
were drawn gradually into the swifter rush of the river.
They approached a ledge where, in unbroken glassy
current, the stream poured over the rock. In they
rushed, and, tilting quickly up on end, made a plunge
like a diver into the seething gulf below. After what
seemed to the spectator several minutes' submergence,
they rose with a bound partially above the surges,
struggling "like some strong swimmer in his agony "
with the stormy waves. Now they rush full tilt
against an iron rock that, mid stream, challenges their
right to pass, and are hurled aside, shuddering, bruised,
and shattered from the encounter. Some are broken
in twain. Others are shivered into splinters. Others
glide by unscathed.

Now one lodges in a narrow channel. Another
strikes and throws it athwart the stream. Then
another and another, and still others in quick succession, lodge, and a formidable "jam" is formed. Now
a huge log careers along like a bolt from a catapult.
It will surely sweep away the obstacle. With a tremendous thud, like the blow of a battering-ram, it
strikes the mass, which quivers, grinds, groans, and
apparently yields a moment, but is faster jammed than
ever. The water rapidly rises and boils and eddies
with tenfold rage.

The "drivers" above have managed to throw a log
across the entrance to the rapid to prevent a further
run, and now set deliberately about loosening the

"jam." With cant-hooks, pike-poles, levers, axes, and ropes, they try to roll, pry, chop, or haul out of the way the logs which are jammed together in a seemingly inextricable mass. The work has a terribly perilous look. The jam may at any moment give way, carrying everything before it with resistless force. Yet these men, who appear almost like midgets as compared with its immense mass, swarm over it, pulling, tugging, shoving, and shouting with the utmost coolness and daring. Like amphibious animals, they wade into the rushing, ice-cold water, and clamber over the slippery logs.

Now an obstructive "stick," as these huge logs are called, is set free. The jam creaks and groans and gives a shove, and the men scamper to the shore. But no ; it again lodges apparently as fast as ever. At work the men go again, when, lo! a single well-directed blow of an axe relieves the whole jam, exerting a pressure of hundreds of tons. It is *sauve qui peut.* Each man springs to escape. The whole mass goes crashing, grinding, groaning over the ledge.

Is everybody safe ? No, Evans has almost got to the shore when he is caught by the heel of his iron-studded boot between two grinding logs. Another moment and he will be swept or dragged down to destruction. Lawrence, not without imminent personal risk, springs forward and catches hold of his outstretched hands. Dowler throws his arms around Lawrence's body, and bracing himself against a rock they all give a simultaneous pull, and the imprisoned foot is freed. And well it is so, for at that moment the whole wrack goes rushing by. The entire occurrence has taken only a few seconds. These lumbermen need to have a quick eye, firm nerves, and strong thews and sinews, for their lives seem often to hang on a hair.

But what is that lithe and active figure dancing down the rapids on a single log, at the tail of the jam ? It is surely no one else than Baptiste la Tour. How

BREAKING THE LOG JAM.

he got there no one knows. He hardly knows himself.
But there he is, gliding down with arrowy swiftness on
a log that is spinning round under his feet with extra-
ordinary rapidity. With the skill of an acrobat or
rope-dancer he preserves his balance, by keeping his
feet, arms, legs, and whole body in constant motion,
the spikes in his boots preventing his slipping. So
long as the log is in deep water and keeps clear of
rocks and other logs, he is comparatively safe.

But see! he will surely run upon that jutting crag!
Nearer and nearer he approaches ; now for a crash and
a dangerous leap! But no! he veers off, the strong
back-wash of the water preventing the collision. Now
the log plunges partly beneath the waves, but by
vigorous struggles he keeps his place on its slippery
surface. Now his log runs full tilt against another.
The shock of the collision shakes him from his feet ;
he staggers and slips into the water, but in a moment
he is out and on his unmanageable steed again.

As he glides out into the smooth water below the
rapids, a ringing cheer goes up from his comrades, who
had been watching with eager eyes his perilous ride.
They had not cheered when the jam gave way, ending
their two hours' strenuous effort. But at Baptiste's
safety irrepressibly their shouts burst forth. With the
characteristic grace of his countrymen, he returned the
cheer by a polite bow, and seizing a floating handspike
that had been carried down with the wrack, he paddled
toward the shore. As he neared it, he sprang from
log to log till he stood on solid ground. Shaking
himself like a Newfoundland dog, he strode up the
bank to receive the congratulations of his comrades.

"That's wuss than breakin' in the breachiest hoss I
ever see," was the comment of Jim Dowler, who spoke
from experience of the latter performance.

"I'd as soon go sailin' on a broomstick wid a witch,
through the air," said Dennis O'Neal, who spoke as if
he had tried that mode of travelling.

"It's better than being caught like an otter in a trap, as I was," said Evans. "I'm like Achilles," he went on, recalling the classic lore he learned at Brasenose, "vulnerable in my heel. But there, I'm sorry to say, the resemblance ends, so far as I can see;" and he laughed a hard, bitter, scornful laugh against himself.

CHAPTER XVI

"THE WORM OF NILUS STINGS NOT SO."

"At the last it biteth like a serpent, and stingeth like an adder."—Prov. xxiii. 32.

"This is an aspic's trail."—SHAKESPEARE: *Ant. and Cleop.*

"Death's harbingers lie latent in the draught,
And in the flowers that wreath the sparkling bowl
Fell adders hiss and poisonous serpents roll."—PRIOR.

LAWRENCE pitied from the bottom of his heart this solitary, cynical, broken-spirited man, who had made shipwreck of such fair prospects, and wasted such golden opportunities, and had sown such a crop of bitter memories, whose melancholy harvest he must now reap. He therefore took an opportunity of quietly conversing with him and endeavouring to inspire hope in his hopeless heart. He referred especially to the good Providence, by which he had been rescued from imminent peril, as a reason why he should endeavour to live a nobler life, and devote his gifts and attainments to the service of God.

"It is very kind of you to care for a poor forlorn wretch whom nobody else cares for; but it's no use, 1 tell you," said Evans. "I know all you would say, and I know it's all true : but it's too late—too late ; "

QUEBEC IN 1887.

CHAMPLAIN STREET IN QUEBEC.

and he gave a heavy sigh. "I've had to make ship-wreck of all that a man should hold dear to be what I am. There was a noble woman loved me once, and I hoped to call her wife, but even her holy influence had not power to keep me from the wine cup." And his features twitched convulsively, and his eyes, though tearless, wore a look of hopeless agony.

"Do you see that log?" he asked, pointing to a bruised and battered trunk drifting helplessly down the rapids. "Well, I am that log, battered and bruised with knocking about in the world, drifting without hope on the stream of chance. Nothing on earth can stop me or help me. It's too late, I tell you," he repeated, with an impatient and almost angry gesture. .

"It is never too late, my brother," said Lawrence, laying his hand affectionately on his arm. "It is never too late, if you will but put your trust in God and look to Him for help."

"It is, for me," said Evans, dejectedly. "Young man, you don't know the overmastering appetite that drives me to drink, as the devil drove the swine into the sea. Here I can't get it, so I keep pretty straight, though an unsatiable craving gnaws at my vitals all the time. But when I go down to Quebec with the raft we are building, I can no more withstand the temptations of the scores of taverns in Champlain Street and *Rue des Matelots* than that log can help going over those falls;" and as he pointed, it disappeared with a plunge in the foam.

"Why, the very smell of the liquor coming out of those low shebeens," he went on, "burns up all my resolutions, as flax is shrivelled in the flames, and I go to my fate like an ox to the slaughter. Even while I think of it the thirst kindles like a tiger's that has tasted blood. You see those boiling rapids? Well, if there was liquor on the other side, I'd go through them to get it."

"O, don't talk so dreadfully!" exclaimed Lawrence, with a shudder. "It is wicked. Try to give it up. Ask God to help you."

"Do you suppose I haven't tried and vowed and prayed?" asked Evans, bitterly. "God only knows how I've tried. But

> 'The limèd soul that struggles to get free
> Is but the more engaged,' .

as the immortal Shakespeare has it; and liquor is the devil's birdlime, by which he catches more souls than by anything else. Young man!" he said, solemnly, grasping Lawrence by the hand, "I'm on my way to hell, and I can't stop; but for God's sake, for your friends' sake, for your soul's sake, I adjure you, never touch the first glass. Would to God I never had;" and he buried his face in his hands.

"I never have, I never will," said Lawrence. "My father taught me when a boy to vow eternal hatred to it, as Hannibal did against the enemies of his country."

"Your father was a wise man," said Evans, raising his head, "and my father was a——, but I'll not upbraid his memory. Yet, when I was a child, he used to have me brought in after dinner, and set me on his knee, and let me sip his wine, and showed me off to his guests, he was so proud of me. He lived to be ashamed enough of me," he added, bitterly.

"And my mother—one of the kindest of mothers, but what mistaken kindness!—when I was studying, used to bring me up wine and cake, and kiss me good-night. I think I see her yet! And, O God! I broke her heart, and brought down my father's grey hairs with sorrow to the grave." And he shuddered through all his frame with a convulsive groan, as he again buried his face in his hands.

Lawrence wept tears of sympathy for this unhappy man, but in the presence of this bitter sorrow, this appalling past and hopeless future, he was dumb.

CHAPTER XVII.

RAFTING.

"The brain grows dizzy with the whirl and hiss
Of the fast-crowding billows as they roll,
Like struggling demons, to the vexed abyss,
Lashing the tortured crags with wild demoniac bliss."
                                        SANGSTER.

THE glorious summertide had come. The leafy
luxuriance of June robed all the forest in richest
verdure. Triliums and sweet wild violets filled the
woods with beauty and fragrance. The river had
fallen to its normal height, and most of the logs had
been run down to join thousands of others on the
mighty flood of the Ottawa. Each bore the brand of
its owner, and they floated on together, to be arrested
by the huge boom, and there sorted out to their several
owners. The long spars and square timber intended
for exportation were made up into "drams," as they
are called. These consist of a number of "sticks" of
pine, oak, elm, or ash, lashed side-by-side. They are
kept together by means of "traverses" or cross pieces,
to which the "sticks" are bound by stout withes of
ironwood or hickory, made supple by being first soaked
in water and then twisted in a machine and wound
around an axle, by which means the fibres are crushed
and rendered pliable. The "drams" are made just

wide enough to run through the timber slides. On the long, smooth reaches of the river they are fastened together so as to make a large raft, which is impelled on its way by the force of the current, assisted by huge oars, and, when the wind is favourable, by sails. In running the rapids, or going through the slides, the raft is again separated into its constituent " drams."

By the end of June all was ready for the final breaking up of the camp. Many of the men had already gone ; some to take up land, others to drive the teams through the forest trail. The last meal was prepared, the personal kit of each man was packed and piled on a raised platform on the raft, and the whole covered with a tarpaulin. On the "Cabin Dram" was built the cook's shanty, with its stores of pork, bread, and biscuit. The raft was loosed from its moorings, and, with a cheer from the men, glided down the stream and out into the Ottawa. It was steered by huge "sweeps" or oars, about twelve yards long. Baptiste and the Indians assumed command of the oars and piloted the raft.

The crew, with but one exception, seemed delighted at the prospect of returning to the precincts of civilization, though to many of them that meant squandering their hard-earned wages in prodigal dissipation and riot. That exception was Matt Evans, who wore the air of a doomed man going to his death.

"I know," he said to Lawrence, "that in a week after we reach Quebec I shall be a drunken vagabond, and not draw a sober breath while my money lasts. I think I'll ship on a two years' whaling voyage. I won't be waylaid by taverns at every turn among the icebergs."

Lawrence was full of eager longing to reach home. He was to leave the raft at Ottawa. Most of the others were to accompany it to Quebec.

The voyage down the river was uneventful, but not monotonous. The weather was glorious. The bright

DOWN AT THE BOOM.

sunlight and pure air seemed to exhilarate like wine.
The raftsmen danced and capered and sang " En roulant
ma boule," and

> "Ah! que l'hiver est long!
> Dans les chantiers nous hivernerons !"

Baptiste meanwhile furnishing the music with his
violin.

Lawrence enjoyed running the rapids exceedingly,
although it was not devoid of a spice of danger. With
the increasing swiftness of the current the water
assumes a glazed or oily appearance. Objects on the
shore fly backward more rapidly. The oars at bow and
stern are more heavily manned. Right ahead are seen
the white seething "boilers" of the rapids. With a
rush the dram springs forward and plunges into the
breakers, which roar like sea monsters for their prey.
The waves break over in snowy foam. The shock
knocks half the men off their feet. They catch hold of
the traverse to avoid being washed overboard. The
dram shudders throughout all its timbers, and the
withes groan and creak as if they would burst asunder
under the strain. The brown rocks gleam through
the waves as they flash past. Soon the dram glides
out into smooth water. The white crested billows race
behind like horrid monsters of Scylla, gnashing their
teeth in rage at the escape of their prey.

The great cauldron of the Chaudière, in which the
strongest dram would be broken like matchwood, was
passed by means of the government timber slides—
long sloping canals, with timber sides and bottoms,
down which the drams glide with immense rapidity.
Sometimes they jam with a fearful collision. But
such accidents are rare.

This is the way in which Canada's great timber
harvest seeks the sea. At Quebec the rafts are
broken up, and the "sticks" are hauled through
timber ports in the bows of the vessels that shall
bear them to the markets of the Old World.

MAKING THE RAFTS.

TIMBER SHIP LEAVING QUEBEC.

CHAPTER XVIII.

"HOME AGAIN."

*"Where er I roam, whatever realms to see,
My heart, untravelled, ever turns to thee."*

GOLDSMITH.

AT Ottawa, Lawrence took leave, not without much emotion, of his winter comrades and friends, for such, with scarce an exception, they had become. He wrung Evans long and warmly by the hand, and adjured him to avoid the taverns at Quebec.

Evans shook his hand and said, " I guess the only safe place for me is at the North Pole, or somewhere else which the liquor has not reached, and such places are hard to find."

O'Neal took both Lawrence's hands in his own and shook them, while the tears ran down his face. "Never fear," he said, "I've drinked my last sup av whisky, an' I'll go an' see the Methody pracher as soon as I get to Quebec, an' put meself under his care. I feel as wake as an unweaned child, not able to walk alone," which, to one who noted his huge bulk and interpreted him literally, would seem a rather astounding statement.

Lawrence received his winter's wages from the agent of the lumber company at Ottawa, and found himself the possessor of more money than he had ever · owned in his life. He felt an honest, manly pride in the fact that it was earned, every dollar, by his own hands. He knew what hard toil it cost, and he determined to make it go as far as possible in carrying out his cherished purpose. The free gift of three times the amount would have been a less valuable possession, without the lessons of thrift, economy, and self-denial that to well-balanced minds hard-earned money brings.

At the camp, on account of his superior education, Evans had been employed much of his time as clerk, accountant, and keeper of the stores. After his accident at the "timber jam," which proved more serious than it seemed at first, Lawrence relieved him of those duties, and had, from his trustworthy character and obliging manner, discharged them greatly to the satisfaction of the foreman and of the entire camp.

Mr. McIntyre, the company's agent, to whom his fidelity and skill had been reported, offered him for three years the post of clerk, which would relieve him of much of the hard work of the camp, with the promise of a hundred dollars increase of salary each year, and the chance of further promotion at the expiration of that time.

"I am much obliged, Mr. McIntyre," replied Lawrence, "but I cannot accept the situation."

"Hae ye onything else in view, lad?" asked the kind-hearted Scotchman.

With some hesitancy Lawrence told him his purpose to use his hard-earned money to pay his way for a time at college.

"Vera guid; I was twa winters at auld Mareschal mysel'. But what then? Ye'll be gangin' into the law or pheesic belike; and enj'yin' genteel starvation instead o' earnin' an honest leevin' in business."

Lawrence modestly explained his further hope of preaching the Gospel.

"An' what'll ye get for that, gin I may speer?" asked the agent.

"Perhaps a hundred dollars a year for four years,"

replied Lawrence, "and then three or four nundred more."

"An' here I offer as much as that at the vera start, and before four years double as much."

"If you were to offer me ten times as much, I dare not take it," said Lawrence firmly, yet respectfully. "I feel bound as by a promise to the dead, a duty to the living, and an obligation to my Maker."

"In that case there's nae mair to be said," replied Mr. McIntyre. "If ye're boun' to starve, ye're gaun to do it on high preenciples, I see. I'll no say ye're no richt. Faur ye weel, an' guid luck to ye;" and he shook him warmly by the hand.

At the truly "general" store of Father Daily Lawrence bought a new suit for himself, stuff for a dress for his mother, and some bright ribbons for little Nell. In spite of himself, he got a very good bargain out of Mr. Daily, who gave him a very unbusiness-like discount. At the village bookstore he bought *Robinson Crusoe* for Tom—a book he had long been wanting—and a copy of Mrs. Hemans' Poems for his sister Mary.

In order to enjoy for a day longer the company of Jim Dowler, to whom he felt his soul knit by tender ties, he took passage in a barge on the Rideau Canal. The little cabin was a mere box "where ye cudn't swing a cat," as Jim remarked. "But then, nobody wants to," he added, "an' so as we can double up at night, what's the odds?"

While the barge was going through the locks, the two friends strolled along the bank of the canal, Lawrence giving much good counsel, and Jim thankfully drinking it in.

"I used to think that nobody cared for Jim Dowler's soul, but now I know better, an' I'll try, God helpin' me, to save it, for yer sake an' my sainted mother's, who's an angel in heaven, an' for my own sake."

At night, they had literally to "double up," so

8

"cabined, cribbed, confined" were they in the berths ·
of the barge. Next morning they parted, Lawrence
taking the stage for Northville. His emotions, as he
drew near home, we shall not attempt to describe. It
was after dark when he arrived. His coming was not
expected, for no letters could be sent from the Mattawa.

He walked rapidly up the garden path, intending to
surprise the inmates ; but the love-quickened ear of
his mother recognised his footstep, and with the cry
of delight, "That's Lawrence ! " she rushed to the door,
scattering spools, thimble, and work on the carpet,—
a homemade one of rags. A moment more and the
brave boy was in his mother's arms, and a long, loving
embrace, holy as any ever known on earth, was his.
His sister Mary claimed her turn, then little Nell and
Tom, who varied the performance by dancing around
the floor with delight, and then returning to hug and
kiss their brother again.

"Thank God to be home again, mother dear," he
said. "I want to embrace you all at once," and he
tried to fold them all in his long, strong arms.

"God bless you, my son ; your mother's prayers are
answered at last."

"How handsome Mary has grown ! " said Lawrence,
after all inquiries as to each other's welfare were over.
"Why, Mary, you're almost as handsome as mother."

"Thank you, Lawrence dear; that's the highest compliment you could pay me," said the affectionate girl.

"And these children, how they've grown ! " he went
on, folding one in each arm. And a very pretty group
they made, the great bronzed fellow, the two fair
children, and the loving mother and sister hanging on
his shoulder and stroking his hair.

"But we must give you more substantial welcome
than this," said the housewifely mother, and soon the
snowy cloth was laid, and furnished with white bread,
sweet butter, and rich strawberries and cream—"A
feast fit for a king," Lawrence declared. While he

did ample justice to this dainty purveying, Tom brought
his slate to show how he could do long division, and
Nelly her Christmas Sunday-school prize, and Mary
her elegant gold watch,—"so useful at school, you
know," she said,—a present for playing the organ in
church ; and the mother brought—well, she had
nothing to bring but the great mother-love beaming
in her rich dark eyes, with which she feasted proudly
on her boy, and he basked in their light with a feeling
of infinite content.

Then the presents were distributed, amid great glee
and fresh caresses—amongst the rest, a pair of em-
broidered moccasins from Red Fawn for his mother,
and tiny bark baskets of maple sugar for the children.
But the bearskin rug made the greatest sensation of
all, and the story of Bruin's capture had to be told
with all its details, the mother's cheek paling, and
Tom's eyes flashing from time to time at the crisis of
the tale. The wolf adventure Lawrence did not tell
for some time after.

Great gladness filled their hearts that night as
Lawrence read his favourite psalm, the hundred and
seventh : "O give thanks unto the Lord, for He is
good; for His mercy endureth for ever," with its
exultant refrain, "O that men would praise the Lord
for His goodness, and for His wonderful works to the
children of men ! " And sound was his sleep and sweet
his dreams as he sank into his pillowy nest in his
little attic chamber, for which he had so often longed
as he lay upon the spruce boughs in the lumber shanty
on the Mattawa. As he lay in the dreamy borderland
between sleeping and waking, he was aware of a
saintly face bending over him, and a mother's kiss
falling lightly as a rose leaf on his forehead, and a
mother's tear, not of sorrow, but of joy, dropping on
his cheek, and he seemed to be again a little child in
his crib, watched over by a mother's love, and his soul
was filled with a great content.

CHAPTER XIX.

OLYMPIC DAYS AND COLLEGE HALLS.

"I passed beside the reverend walls
  In which of old I wore the gown;
  I roved at random through the town,
And saw the tumult of the halls."
                    TENNYSON : *In Memoriam.*

'For him was lever han, at his beddes head,
  Twenty bokes clothed in black and red,
  Of Aristotle and his philosophie,
  Than robes riche, or fidel, or sautrie :
  Of studie took he most cure and hede.
  Not a word spake he more than was nede;
  Souning in moral vertue was his speche;
  And gladly wolde he lerne, and gladly teche."
                    CHAUCER : *Canterbury Tales.*

THIS peaceful episode in his life Lawrence regarded but as the arbour on the Hill Difficulty, in which he might rest for a while to brace his energies for future toil. He resolved, therefore, that its delights should not enervate his soul. He wrote accordingly the very next day to the Rev. Dr. Fellows, the President of Burghroyal College, asking for the "course of study" and such advice as he might be able to give. Meanwhile, he hunted up among his father's books those that he thought would be useful, and applied himself with renewed zeal to his Greek Testament and grammar. He won golden opinions from the Northville farmers by going into the haying and harvest fields and earning honest wage for honest work.

In a few days came a kind letter from Dr. Fellows, giving the desired information, and some wise counsel, not unmixed with the Attic salt of wit. Lawrence had learned to do what he did with his might—the best lesson that any young man can learn—the key that will unlock all difficulties and open every avenue to success. He therefore worked hard at his books and in the field, with sweat of brain and sweat of brow, till the time approached to leave home. for college. This parting was a comparatively easy task ; for, could he not write home every week? and return at Christmas, or in a single day, if need were ?

The Burghroyal College is the mental Mecca of many an ambitious Canadian youth—the objective point to which, like Lawrence Temple, they struggle through many difficulties. It has been the *Alma Mater*, tender and beloved, which has nourished and brought up many sons, who in all parts of our broad Dominion rise up and call her blessed. As Lawrence approached this venerable seat of learning—venerable in its dignity and high character, as well as, for a young country, venerable in point of age—his heart beat high with hope. He had reached the goal of long months, almost years, of struggle—the starting-place, also, in a new race for knowledge and wider range for usefulness.

As he approached the town, the setting sun shone brightly on the conspicuous cupola of the college, which beamed like a star of promise in the heavens, beckoning him onward, as it seemed to him, to a higher plane of being. As he ascended the massive stone steps and passed beneath the lofty and pillared portico of the building, he felt like a Greek neophyte entering the temple of Pallas Athene.

The following day he presented himself to Dr. Dwight, who had charge of the domestic and moral government of the institution, as Dr. Fellows had of its literary department. He was a man to arrest attention anywhere—tall, straight as a Norway pine, with clear-cut features, expressive of great promptness and energy of character, and with an alertness of manner and action that seemed to belong to a younger man than he appeared to be. Lawrence felt a little awed as he stood in his presence, but the Doctor frankly held out his hand and said,

"Ah, Temple, I'm glad to see you; I heard you were coming." He always seemed somehow to hear everything and to know everything pertaining to the college.

The doctor looked sharply at him for a moment with those keen eyes that seemed to read his very thoughts.

"I knew your father, Temple, and respected him highly," he continued; "you are like him in person: I can wish nothing better for you than to be like him in character."

These words made Lawrence thrill with pleasure, and he resolved more firmly than ever to be worthy of that father's memory and reputation.

The Doctor then inquired kindly as to the young student's plans and purposes, in which he evinced a fatherly sympathy and interest.

"Where have you been during the year?" he asked in his alert manner.

Lawrence briefly recounted his adventures on the Mattawa.

"Good! I admire your pluck," said the Doctor: "I congratulate you on having to depend on yourself. It is worth more than a fortune to you. Hew your way for yourself here, as you did among the big trees on the Mattawa, and it will develop a strength of character that will carry you anywhere and enable you to do anything. It is well for a man to bear the yoke in his youth. It will give him the shoulders

and strength of Atlas. Steward, show Mr. Temple
to his room, please ; " and turning to that functionary,
he designated the apartment which Lawrence was to
occupy.

" What a general he would make!" thought Lawrence
as he left the Doctor's presence ; " I could follow that
man anywhere." He already felt the inspiration of his
character. " But I would like to be sure that I was
always right," he further reflected, as he remembered
the keen scrutiny of that commanding glance.

His room was a pleasant apartment, affording a
magnificent view over the broad lake and the pretty
town in which the college was situated. A bed, table,
chairs, and washstand constituted its simple furniture ;
but when his books were unpacked and placed on
shelves, their familiar faces made it look quite home-
like.

Soon after, he called on Dr. Fellows for advice in
his studies, and was very courteously received. The
Doctor was a very noticeable sort of man, who somehow put Lawrence in mind of pictures he had seen of
Andrea Dandolo, one of the doges of Venice in the days
of her mediæval prime. He had the same lofty brow,
handsome face, clear olive complexion, quick insight
of glance, and general scholarly air. In his brief conversation with Lawrence, he seemed equally at home
in ancient and in modern lore, in poetry and philosophy.
He impressed the young student as his ideal of a
scholar—though learned, simple and unaffected ; his
words, though weighted with wisdom, flashing oftentimes with wit, like a robe of rich texture bejewelled
with sparkling gems.

In the great dining-room, filled with eager, active,
hungry youth,—for college boys have most portentous
appetites,—Lawrence felt more lonely than even amid
the forest solitudes of the Mattawa. One is often
never so much alone as in a crowd. It was a severe
ordeal to his retiring disposition to encounter the in-

quiring glances and sometimes critical stare of so many
young men, all of whom, he thought, knew so much
more than himself.   The acquaintance formed with his
table companions somewhat reassured him, by showing
that they were very much like ordinary mortals,—that
human nature even in college halls differs not very
greatly from human nature in a lumber camp.

Nothing so breaks the ice of formality as a good
laugh, and this experience Lawrence enjoyed at his
first college meal.   It was the usage for the whole
company to wait for the slowest eater to finish his
meal—sometimes a little impatiently, for college boys
are too apt to bolt their food and hurry back to ball
or cricket.   On this occasion an unlucky individual,
who was " slow but sure," kept the tables waiting an
undue time.   As he finished his dessert, the wag of
the college, who was sitting near him, a tall, shambling,
awkward-looking fellow with ill-fitting clothes, but
with a merry twinkle in his eye that made him a
general favourite, assuming a dignified, forensic air,
slightly accommodating to the occasion the memorable
reply of Pitt to Horace Walpole, asked, " Is the gentleman done ?   Is he quite done ?   He has been voracious
from beginning to end."

It was not very much of a joke, but Lawrence found
it impossible to avoid joining in the laugh which it
caused.

It was not long before he also had experience of the
supreme disdain and lofty, supercilious airs with which
certain gentlemen of the sophomore year regarded the
newly admitted freshmen, assuming far more dignity
than the graduating class.   He felt greatly abashed
at this, till he discovered that their knowledge was not
quite so encyclopædic as they thought, although they
seemed to know so much more than the professors
themselves.   Some of the city lads, too, put on somewhat extensive airs on account of the more dandified
cut of their coats as compared with their country cousins'

But a college class-room is a great leveller. No-where are windbags more easily pricked, or do they more suddenly collapse. A professor is no respecter of persons. Money gives no monopoly of brains, and the poor students, for the most part, win the prizes by virtue of the energy of character developed by the very effort they have to make to gain an education.

In the Greek class one day, one of these dainty gentlemen was most effectually taken down. Professor Nelson, a mild-mannered gentleman, who sat quietly behind his gold glasses and seemed to take little note of aught but the text book before him—but those who attempted to take any liberties would find out their mis-take—called on Mr. Adolphus Fitztomkyns to recite. That gentleman started, hesitated, stopped, and fumbled his gold chain, amid the sustained silence of the Professor.

At length, " I do not know what ἤλακα is from," he said.

" It is from ἐλαύνω," said the Professor.

Another pause. " I don't know what part it is," said the embarrassed youth.

" The perfect," replied Dr. Nelson, without the least accent of asperity in his tone.

Another long pause of awful solemnity, in which the beaded sweat stood on the youth's forehead. At last in desperation he made the honest confession, " I know nothing about it," and sat down.

Not a word was uttered, but the unhappy lad felt the unspoken reproach more keenly than the sternest reproof.

Professor Rexton, however, who had an utter abhor-rence of sham, seemed to take a special delight in displacing fools from their pedestal of conceit. His department, too, that of mathematics, supplied some-times salient opportunities of doing this. There was no room for imperfect recitations or illogical reasoning there. The habits of rigid accuracy acquired by this

means were invaluable in their result.   The lofty principles of mathematics and their sublime applications
in astronomy were a keen delight to Lawrence.'

His greatest pleasure, however, was to wander
through the woods or by the shore of the lake, with its
remarkable geological outcrop, with Professor Wash-
burn, the young and enthusiastic instructor in natural
science.   Breaking off twigs from the trees as he
walked, the latter would point out the beautiful mor-
phology of the leaves, and their wonderful phyllotaxis
—the mathematical exactness with which they are
arranged in spirals around their stem.   Or, knocking
an encrinite or coral out of the corniferous rock, he
would discourse luminously of the bygone geologic
ages.   Then he would advance to the constitution and
genesis of the universe, and, rising from Nature up to
Nature's God, would reason on the lofty themes of

"Fixed fate, free will, foreknowledge absolute,"

and the glorious truths of atonement and redemption.

Lawrence seemed to himself to drink in knowledge
at every pore—to acquire it by all his senses.   He
seemed to feel new faculties developing within, as the
dull chrysalis may feel the wings of Psyche forming
under its coat.   In the Burghroyal College, learning
was not divorced from religion, nor science made the
handmaid of scepticism.   All the resources of knowledge were brought to the illustration and corroboration
of God's revealed truth; and every effort was made
to cultivate in the young men a manly rational piety
which would enable its possessors to give a reason for
the hope that was in them.

The influence of our colleges on the future of our
country is of incalculable importance.   They will
either curse it with scepticism or bless it with piety.
In those college halls are assembled, at the most
impressible and formative period in their history, the
most eager, active, energetic, and ambitious young men

of our country,—the future legislators, judges, lawyers, physicians, professors, editors, teachers, and preachers of the future. Upon what they shall be depends the destiny of our country.

If the majority of them become materialistic sceptics, denying the God Who made them, the Lord Who bought them, and the spiritual nature with which He endowed them, the age shall be a coarse, vulgar, venal, and sensual one. Knowledge shall be a bane, not a blessing—a power indeed, but for evil, not for good. If, on the contrary, they be men of faith in God and His Word, of high-souled principles and of spiritual instincts, then shall they guide the age as a skilful rider guides his steed up the heights of progress to a higher plane of being, a wider range of thought, a purer moral atmosphere, and a nobler type of life.

CHAPTER XX.

ON THE THRESHOLD.

LAWRENCE found his religious advantages and helps much greater than he had anticipated, if we may judge from the following extract from a letter, which about this time he wrote home:

"I am agreeably disappointed in more than one respect with the college, and especially with the religious atmosphere which seems to pervade the institution. I thought the reverse would be the case, from the stories that Tom Brown, who was rusticated two years ago, used to tell us about the pranks that he and his chums used to play on the religious students —knocking down the blackboards and putting out the lights at their prayer-meetings, locking them in their rooms, and then stopping up the chimneys so as to smoke them out.

"Tom Potter, my classmate, and a first-rate fellow, says these are all traditions of the prehistoric age. Nobody here knows anything about them; and that story about taking the cow up the stairway and fastening her to the bell-rope, which she is said to have kept tolling all night, I believe is a sheer fabrication of Brown's. I cannot find any foundation for it in fact.

"The professors are very kind—more like friends

than teachers. I thought I would have more persecution to encounter from the wild collegians than I
had among the lumbermen on the Mattawa. But I
have had none at all, but, on the contrary, much
sympathy from religious students and much help from
the professors. Dr. Nelson has a Bible Class every
week, and brings all his classic lore to the explanation
of the Scriptures. Then I read the Greek Testament
with him, and have begun Hebrew. Dear Doctor
Whitcombe is almost like a father. He introduced
me very kindly to the class, and they all rose to receive
me. And he bows so politely to each student as they
enter the class-room. He is a wonderful old philosopher—a sort of Friar Bacon among his retorts and
alembics. He talks as familiarly about molecules and
atoms as if he had been handling them all his life.

"I see almost as little of the fair sex here as at the
Mattawa. Good old Mrs. McDonnell, the matron, is
the only one I have spoken to. She is a stately old
lady, but a kind, motherly soul. She came to see
me when I was confined to my room with a cold. I
am a regular hermit. ' I bury myself in my books, and '
—I'll not finish the quotation ; Mary may look for it
in Tennyson's *Maud*, if she likes.

"We have grand meetings on Saturday night—the
students by themselves—though sometimes some of
the professors look in. Then we have such singing.
There are several young preachers here—the finest set
of young fellows you ever saw—and instead of college
life killing their piety, as old Squire Jones says it will,
it seems to kindle it into a brighter flame. So many
burning embers together make a hot fire. One of
them, James Thompson, is my class-leader—a dear,
good soul. The tears will stream down his cheeks
when he is talking to us.

"The Greeks, when they were very fortunate, used
to sacrifice to Nemesis, to deprecate her anger. If I
were a Greek, I might do so too, for truly the lines

have fallen to me in very pleasant places.   But I will
fear no evil in the future, but give thanks to God for
His great goodness.
                    " Ever your loving
                                    " LAWRENCE."

Lawrence did not encounter much persecution, it is
true, but he was not without sundry petty annoyances.
    " Where did you learn to swing your axe so scientifi-
cally ? " asked a dandified city youth who was always
grumbling at the rule which required the students to
cut their own fuel.
    " Where they understand the science, in a lumber
camp on the Mattawa," said Lawrence, civilly.
    " The Mattawa! where's that ? " asked his inter-
locutor, whose knowledge of the geography of his
own country was rather at fault.
    Lawrence good-naturedly explained.
    " So you're a common lumberman! " sneered the
ill-bred rowdy—for such he was, despite his fine clothes.
" What right have the like of you to come to college
among gentlemen ?   I suppose it's to pay your board
you ring the bell at six o'clock on winter mornings."
    "Precisely so," replied Lawrence, calmly, " and
I am not ashamed of it either.   Poverty is no crime,
but rude insolence is," he added, with some asperity.
• He felt stung by the impertinence from one who wore
the garb and claimed the character of a gentleman.
But no bully is more brutal than your aristocratic
bully.   He felt vexed at himself for letting such a
creature have power to sting his feelings.   He

          " Scorned to be scorned by one that he scorned,"

but he remembered the words of Byron, " The kick
of an ass will give pain to one to whom its most
exquisite braying will give no pleasure."
    " Temple," said Dr. Dwight, one day, in his brisk
manner, " I wish you would take charge of that boy,

young Elliot. I forewarn you, he is a little wasp.
Nobody else will room with him, but I think *you* can.
I believe you will do him good, and I am sure he will
do you good. ' Let patience have her perfect work,'
you know ! "

"I'll try, sir," said Lawrence, flattered by the good
opinion expressed, but not very confident of success.

The little urchin had gone the round of the rooms
of all the older students, and worn out their patience
in succession. He deliberately set himself, like a
young monkey, by all kinds of mischievous pranks, to
exhaust the patience of Lawrence. But that commodity might in this case be fitly represented by
the unknown quantity x. It seemed literally inex-
haustible.

The poor boy was a "mitherless bairn," brought up
among hirelings, and he had consequently grown up
into a petty tyrant. Lawrence pitied and yearned
over the lad, and secretly prayed for him. He helped
him in his algebra and Latin exercises, gave him
pence to buy marbles, brought him fruit from the
country, and, in fact, overcame his ill temper with
kindness. Before long he had no more ardent cham-
pion than the young scapegrace, as he was considered,
Tom Elliot. He would fetch and carry for Lawrence
like a dog, and demonstrated the grand fact that under
the warmth of human lovingkindness the iciest nature
will melt—the sternest clod will blossom with beauty
and affection.

Lawrence was anxious to do some good in the community in which he lived ; so he organized a syste-
matic tract distribution from house to house in the
town, omitting none. He was generally very favour-
ably received, especially among the poor fishermen,
and felt great pleasure in his work and in the opportunity of speaking a word for the Master to some
toil-worn woman or disheartened man, and of gathering
the little children into his class in Sunday school.

One surly fellow, however, passionately tore his tract
in two and lit his pipe with it, saying :

" Look-a-here, mister, I don't want none o' yer trac's
about yer, except those you make right straight away
from this house. Ef ye come round yer agin', I'll set
that dog on to ye," pointing to an ugly bulldog.
" He can fight anythin' his heft in the country, an'
he'll tear ye wuss nor I tore yer trac'. So make tracks
now. Clear ! vamose ! I tell ye."

Lawrence bade him ·a polite good-morning and
passed on.

More disheartening, however, was the stony, gorgo-
nizing stare and the icy politeness that he encountered
from a fine lady at a grand house in the " swell" part
of the town. Resolved, however, not to be deterred
from his duty, he called again at both houses on the
next Sunday.

"You here agin !" said his burly antagonist. "What
did I tell yer ? Well, ye're grit, I must say. May yer
leave a trac' ? I s'pose ther's no denyin' yer. Give
it to the 'ooman thar ;" and Lawrence gladly left a
message of consolation to the poor draggled-looking
creature in the cabin.

At the grand house the stare was less stony, and
the ice somewhat thawed. In the course of time it
melted entirely away, and the stare relaxed into a
smile.

The quarterly meeting of the Burghroyal Church,
of which Lawrence proved an active member, soon
placed him on the local preachers' plan, and he had
frequent opportunity of exercising his gifts and graces
in preaching at numerous outposts of Methodism in
the beautifully undulating and rich farming country
in the vicinity of the town. Such evidence of success,
adaptation, and Divine call to this work did he mani-
fest, that he was unanimously recommended by the
Board to be taken on trial as a Methodist preacher.

Though he would gladly have remained longer at

college, the demand for young men to enter opening doors of usefulness in the newer parts of the country, his own burning zeal to work for the Master, and the inadequacy of his purse to defray college expenses, without being a burden to loved ones at home—one which they would gladly bear, but which Lawrence would not suffer to be imposed—all these conspired to make it desirable that he should go out into the work, if accepted, immediately after the following Conference.

The last night of the session had arrived, the examinations were ended, and the busy scenes of the Convocation week were over. The latter was quite a brilliant and, to Lawrence, a novel occasion. The Faculty, wearing their professorial robes, with the distinguished visitors, filled the dais. The gownsmen and spectators thronged the floor—the ladies raining sweet influence from their eyes on the young aspirants for fame. The Latin oration, the Greek ode, the English valedictory were all given with great *éclat*. Dr. Fellows, looking like a Venetian Doge in his robes of state, had conferred the degrees on the *Baccalaurei* and *Magistri Artium*. Each on bended knee placed his hands, pressed palm to palm, between those of the President, in pledge of fealty to his *alma mater*, and received the investiture of his Bachelor's or Master's hood, like a youthful knight of olden time being girded with his sword for chivalric devoir for the right against the wrong.

Lawrence would gladly have pursued, like a young athlete, this classic *cursus*, but, at the claims of what he considered to be a higher duty, he was content to forego it. Nevertheless, he declared that he would not take a thousand dollars—more money than he had ever seen, poor fellow—for what he had already learned. And he was right. He had, at least, laid the foundation for building thereon the goodly structure of a sound and comprehensive education—which

9

is the work of a lifetime, always advancing, never completed.

On this last night Lawrence walked beneath the trees in the moonlight and the starlight, with his room-mate and devoted chum, Tom Elliot, exchanging vows of mutual affection and pledges of eternal friendship. The old college was brilliantly lighted up. A band of music was discoursing classic strains on the lawn. A supper of an unusually festive character was spread in the ample dining-room. Exchanges of cards and farewells were taking place. A tinge of pensive melancholy blended with the joyousness of the occasion. O golden time, when youths, trained by literary culture and Christian influences, stand on the threshold of life—looking back on the bright and happy boyhood that is passed, looking forward to the duties and joys of manhood that are before them— eager to

"Drink delight of battle with their peers"

in the conflict of life into which, like gallant knights fresh from the accolade, they long to rush.

The next day they were all scattered far and wide, and the college halls, so lately vocal with the din of eager, happy voices, were silent almost as the ruins of Nineveh.

Lawrence abode quietly at home, awaiting trustfully the decision of Conference as to his future destiny. He accepted his three weeks' furlough, like a soldier on the eve of a campaign. To his mother it was a great delight to have him home again. The Augustine and Monica communings were renewed, and a proud joy was it for that happy mother to walk to church leaning on her son's strong arm, and to listen to his voice as he occupied the pulpit in the place of the minister who was absent at Conference. It carried her back to the early days of her marriage —he looked so like his father in his youth—and if she closed her eyes, she could hardly resist the illusion that it was that voice, so long silent, that she heard.

The kindly neighbours, at the close of the service, greeted them both with great warmth.

"A peart boy that o' yourn," said old Squire Jones to the widow. "I'm powerful glad to see that college larnin' hasn't spilt him. He's jes' as plain-talkin' as his father afore him, that never see'd the inside of a college. A chip o' the old block, he is; got rale preacher's timber into him, an' no mistake."

During the week came a letter from Mr. Turner, his "Chairman," stating that he had been duly received by the Conference and appointed to a mission in the Muskoka region, then newly opened to settlement. "It's a rather rough region," wrote Mr. Turner, "but it's not worse than many a circuit your father had, and I knew that his son would not shrink from the task."

"When I gave myself to the Methodist Church," was Lawrence's comment to his mother, "I gave myself to it for life, not to pick and choose for myself, but to go wherever the voice of the Church, which to me is the voice of God, sends me. I can go out like Abraham, not knowing whither I go, but knowing that God will go with me and prepare my way before me."

"That is the way I married your father, Lawrence," said his mother, pressing her lips to his forehead, "for better, for worse, for richer, for poorer; and, amid all our trials, I never for a moment had cause to regret it. The God of your father will be also your God, my son."

During the few days that remained before his departure, the brave mother kept up her heart in his presence, though she often retired to her little chamber to pray, and sometimes to weep—to weep mingled tears of joy and regret—of joy that the vow of consecration at his birth was fulfilled, that she was

permitted to give him to the holiest work on earth—
of natural regret at losing such a son. She followed
him about with wistful eyes, which were sometimes
filled with tears. But her time was fully occupied in
finishing a set of shirts for her boy, at which his sister
Mary diligently helped. Even the irrepressible Tom
and frolicsome Nelly seemed as if they never could do
enough for him.

As he parted from his mother in the porch, he
whispered, " Remember me, dear mother, at the throne
of grace, especially on Sunday morning. I shall go
to my appointments more full of faith if I know that
you are praying for me."

" I will, my son. I always did for your father, and
he said it helped him. God bless you, my boy ; " and
she kissed him good-bye. As he departed with the
seal of that mother's kiss upon his brow, and the
peace and joy of God in his heart, he felt that life's
highest and holiest ambition was reached—that he
was indeed the " King's Messenger," and that he
went forth a herald of salvation, an ambassador of
God, to declare to perishing men the glorious tidings
of the Gospel of His grace.

SAWMILL IN THE FOREST.

ON THE HEAD WATERS OF THE SEVERN.

CHAPTER XXI.

IN THE FIELD.

'How beautiful upon the mountains are the feet of him that bringeth good tidings!"—ISA. lii. 7.

" Oft did the harvest to their sickle yield.
    Their furrow oft the stubborn glebe has broke;
How jocund did they drive their teams a-field!
    How bowed the woods beneath their sturdy stroke!

"' Let not ambition mock their useful toil,
    Their homely joys, and destiny obscure;
Nor grandeur hear with a disdainful smile
    The short and simple annals of the poor."
                          GRAY—*Elegy*.

LAWRENCE took the steamer to Toronto, in which city he spent a day. The wide streets, the moving multitudes, the number and elegance of the churches, were to him a novel spectacle, bringing a stronger sense of the bigness of the world than even the wilderness of the Mattawa. While making his frugal purchases of books at the Wesleyan Book Room, in whose purlieu the preachers most do congregate, and which contained more volumes than he had ever seen before, the minister of one of the city churches claimed him as a lawful prize, and carried him off to share his hospitality and preach in the evening.

The next day he proceeded by railway to Barrie, and thence by steamer again to the pretty village of Orillia. Here he took the stage for Muskoka. He had an ominous initiation into his work. The road was of frightful ruggedness. The old earth showed her bones in a huge out-crop of primeval granite, with scarcely soil enough to decently cover her nakedness. Lawrence had to cling to his seat as the rough strong stage climbed the rugged ridges and rattled down the other side, like a landsman in a ship on a stormy sea. At last, in descending a steep hill, the horses could no longer hold back, and the stage, rattling to the bottom, came to grief against a huge stone. There was nothing for it but to walk to his destination, some half-dozen miles further, carrying his valise in his hand. The road became less rugged, but the heat was excessive, and the black-flies and mosquitoes were a perfect plague.

" Be you the noo preacher ? " asked an honest-faced, sunburnt, tan-freckled man, as Lawrence wearily trudged up to the post-office, store, and principal building generally of the little village of Centreville—though it was not very apparent of what it was the centre. The speaker was dressed in grey homespun trousers, which looked very warm for the season, a grey flannel shirt, coarse boots, and a broad-brimmed straw hat, with ample means for ventilation in its crown. A fringe of sandy hair surrounded his broad, honest face, as he beamed welcome on the new-comer.

"Oi'm the çarcuit stooard," he went on, when Lawrence owned the soft impeachment; "jes' come along with me. We wuz expectin' of yer. Jes' let me have yer baggage. I see the black-flies 'a' been givin' yer a Muskoka welcome," calling Lawrence's attention to the fact that the blood was streaming down his neck from their bites—a circumstance of which he had not been aware. Soon, however, he was very painfully reminded of it, for the bites began to swell and to become exceedingly inflamed.

"They allers do take to strangers," said the circuit official. "Ye'll hev to get some ile and smear your face with it—fish ile's the best."

"Are they so bad as that?" inquired Lawrence in some trepidation, for he had a constitutional aversion to the touch of any kind of oil.

"Well, they do say they killed a man out north here; but I guess that wuz a kind o' drawin' a long bow. Somethin' like the story 'bout our muskeeters. Yer know, they say many on 'em will weigh a pound."

"They don't say how many, though," said Lawrence, who saw through the joke.

"Yer'll do for Muskoka, I reckon, if yer allers as cute as that," said the steward admiringly. "We want a pretty peart man in here, I till yer. A'most anybody 'll do for outside, but it takes a *man* to get along in here, it doos."

"Excuse me, Mr. Steward ; I have not the pleasure of knowing your name yet," said Lawrence.

"Hophni Perkins, at yer sarvice," replied that functionary with a galvanic attempt at a bow.

"Hophni! what a singular name. I never heard it out of the Bible before."

"Well, yer see," explained Mr. Perkins, "father and mother, they wuz old fashioned Methodis' out to the front, and they wuz great on Scriptooral names. So they called my twin brother Phinehas—he lives jes' over the swale yonder—and they had to call me Hophni, to keep up the balance, I s'pose. They mought a' chosen more respectabler namesakes for us, though. Hows'ever, that don't make no odds. It's somethin' like original sin, I 'low. A man ain't jedged fer the name he bears, an' I won't be punished fer Hophni's sins, but fer my own, unless they is washed away in the blood o' the Lamb. An', praise the Lord, mine is. I've got the assurance every day. But here we are," he continued, as they reached a small log cabin standing near the roadside. The chimney was built of sticks and clay, but the evening meal was being cooked out-of-doors, gipsy-fashion, as was the general custom in hot weather.

"Jerushy, here's the noo preacher," he said to a toil-worn, weary-looking woman in a woolsey petti-coat and linen upper-garment of no distinctive name.

"Yer welcome, shure," she said, rising from the frying-pan where she was cooking a savoury meal, a kindly smile illuminating her plain features.

"Yer to make this yer home till quarterly meetin'," said Mr. Perkins, "then they'll arrange where yer to go. It'll be month about, I guess, beginnin' at Brother Phin's over there. We call him that fer short, yer know. Yer may find some places better'n this, but yer'll find more wuss. Set down, set down. Yer must be hungry. Jerushy, what have yer got? Where's the childer?"

"Tom caught some bass in the lake," said that woman of few words, but of kind heart and acts. The children, brown as young Indians and timid as fawns, were hiding around the corner of the house, recon-noitring the new-comer, but the attractions of the supper brought them one by one to the table. As this was the new preacher's first meal, a tablecloth, clean but coarse, was spread—a luxury not always thought necessary on subsequent occasions. The fish was delicious. The same could hardly be said of the chips of pork floating in a sea of fat. The butter and milk were fresh and rich, but the tea was not of the finest aroma. The wild strawberries and cream, how-ever, were "fit for a king," said Lawrence.

· After prayers with this kind family, hospitable to the extent of their means—and a king could be no more—Lawrence was shown to his sleeping apart-ment. It was a loft under the roof, to which access was had by means of a rude ladder in the corner.

"We go to roost with the fowls, and get up with the fowls here," said Mr. Perkins.

"Look out fer yer head," he added, just *after* Lawrence had brought that important part in contact with the low rafter. A faint light came through a small four-pane window, which was open for ventilation. The furniture of the loft consisted of a flock bed, a spinning-wheel, a quantity of wool which had a strong greasy smell, tied up in a blanket, and a quantity of last year's corn in the cob, lying on the floor.

Lawrence slept the sleep of youth, of peace of mind and of a weary body. He woke early, but found that the household were stirring before him. For want of other means of making his ablutions, he washed in a tin basin set on the end of the large trough out of doors, although it was raining slightly, and dried his hands and face on a roller towel behind the door. Having forgotten to provide himself with a comb and brush, which useful articles he procured on his first visit to the store, he tried to arrange his dishevelled locks with a lead-pencil—not, however, with a very high degree of success. Looking-glass, that luxury of civilization, there was none, except a small disc not much larger than a watch hanging on the wall, before which Mr. Perkins performed his weekly shaving operation. To get a view of his broad face in its small surface, he was obliged to twist his features as though he were making faces for a wager, and to squint sideways in a manner that threatened permanent strabismus. Notwithstanding these efforts, or perhaps in consequence of them, he sometimes nicked his features in a manner by no means ornamental, especially as he employed as a styptic a film of cobweb which contrasted strongly with his ruddy countenance and snowy but unstarched expansive shirt collar.

Next day Mr. Perkins accompanied Lawrence "cross lots" to introduce him to Jeremiah Hawkins, or "Jerry Hawkins" as he was generally called, the

class-leader of the Centreville appointment. They
found him ploughing in a field with a lean horse and
a cow yoked together. He was a little meagre old
man with bright eyes like a ferret.

"Brother Hawkins, this is the noo preacher," said
Mr. Perkins, making the introduction with the very
essence of true politeness, though without some of its
outward forms.

The old man took from his head a well-worn musk-
rat fur cap, in places rubbed bare, which, notwithstanding the intense heat of the weather, he wore, and
pulling his iron-grey forelock made what might be
described as a strongly-accented bow.

"Put on your cap, Father Hawkins," said Lawrence,
warmly shaking his hand. "I never like an old man
to uncover to me. I feel that I ought rather to take
off my hat to him."

"An' thoo be the noo praicher, bless the Lord!"
said Father Hawkins, leaning against his plough
handle. "Oi wor afeared the Conference wouldn'
send us none—we'me raised so little for the last. But
we'me did what we'me could, didn't us, Hophni?"

"Yes, but the times wuz bad. We'll do better to
year," said that hopeful individual.

"O! the Conference will not throw you over because you're poor," said Lawrence cheerily. "And
the Missionary Board will do what they can. That's
what the Missionary Society is for, to help those that
can't help themselves."

"It would al-to break we're hearts to have no
praichin' nor ordinances, wouldn't it, Hophni?" said
the old man.

"That it would," said Mr. Perkins. "When I
com'd in here, an' my little Isaac wuz born, ther
wuzn't no preacher to baptize him, an' when he died
ther wuzn't none within forty miles to bury him. An'
my Jerushy, she took on so 'cause the poor child had
never been christened. She wuz Piscopalian, yer

know, an they makes great account o' that. But we digged a grave in the corner o' the lot. An' Father Hawkins here, he said a prayer an' exhorted a bit over the little coffin, an' then we carried him out an' buried him; an' I believe the angels watch his sleep jes' as much as though it wuz in ever so consecrated groun'."

"Not a doubt of it," said Lawrence, "their angels do always behold the face of our Father in heaven."

"You're from Devonshire," he continued to Father Hawkins, knowing that one can always draw people out by speaking of their native place.

"Yes. Be thoo?" said the old man brightening up. "But thoo hast na getten they speach."

"No," said Lawrence, with a patriotic emotion, "I'm from a better place, I'm a Canadian."

"Na, na, lad, thoo canst na be frae a better place, though we'me na runnin' doon Canada. But thoo've never seen they green lanes of Devon, an' they orchards, an' they hop-fields, an' they rich lush pastur', an' they Devonshire cream. Hav' 'em, Hophni?" and the old man sighed as he contrasted the rich culture of that garden county of the old land with the raw newness of the rocky region to which in his old age he was transplanted, like one of the hop vines of his native shire, torn up by the roots and planted on a rock.

"Canada's not such a bad place to be born in after all," said Mr. Perkins.

"The best in the world," interjected Lawrence.

"When father com'd to York township, on the front, fifty year agone, there wuz no roads no more'n here. An' the mud wuz that bad cattle got mired every spring. An' now we'll soon have the railroad an' steamboats an' the market brought to our very doors."

Father Hawkins proceeded to give Lawrence a list of the names and residences of the members of the

Centreville class, which he kept in his head, because,
poor man, he couldn't " read writing, or reading either
for that matter." It was for this purpose, indeed, that
the latter called upon him.

There was old " Widdah Beddoes " up the river;
and her son and his wife, they lived on the lake road ;
and Squire Hill, " kep' the store and Pos' Office ; "
and Brother Jones, the local preacher, lived above the
Big Falls.

" Good fishin' up thar ef yer that ways inclined,"
remarked Mr. Perkins.

Lawrence admitted that he was not much of a
sportsman.

" No more ain't I," replied his host. " Fishin' only
fit for boys. Men's time's too precious. I kin arn
more in a day on the farm than I could catch fish in
a week. It may do for city gents who can afford to
come out yer with all their fancy tackle an' catch fish
that cost 'em 'bout four dollars a-piece ; but a man as
works for his livin' can't afford it."

We imagine that our forest philosopher spoke with
a good deal of truth.

" Thoo kin 'ave ma boaat for visitin' they foaks up
t' river an' along t' lake : an' fer the upper 'pintment,
Squire Hill 'll lend thoo his meer, when her's no
woakin'. But fer the rest, Oi suspect thoo'll 'ave
to use shanks' meer, as we'me used to call it in oor
parts."

This good old man had been selected for the important office of class-leader and guiding souls to heaven,
it was evident, not for his wealth or social influence
or learning, but on account of his possession of the
highest and most essential qualification—his sincere
and fervid piety. Although he could not read a word,
his mind was stored with Scripture and with Wesley's
hymns. In class he would bring out of his treasury
things new and old, exhorting, warning, encouraging,
reproving, in the spirit of meekness and love. And

FALLS OF THE SEVERN, MUSKOKA.

BACKWOODS POST OFFICE.

LOADING LOGS.

he would pray with such fervour that all hearts
were first melted and then kindled to a glow of holy
zeal.

"Two men I honour," says Carlyle—we quote from
memory—"and no third. First, the man that with
earth-made implement conquers the earth and makes
her man's. Venerable to me is the hard hand, crooked
and coarse. Thou art in the path of duty, my brother,
be out of it who may. Thou art toiling for the altogether indispensable, for daily bread.

"Another man I honour," he continues, "and still
more highly—him who toils for the spiritually indispensable, for the bread of life. Unspeakably touching
is it when both these dignities are united ; when he
who is toiling outwardly for the lowest of men's wants
is toiling inwardly for the highest. Sublimer know I
nothing than such a peasant-saint, could such now
anywhere be met with."

Such, we make bold to assert, are many of the
humble, toiling class-leaders and local preachers of
the Methodist Church, who imitate in their daily walk
the Blessed Life which was lived in Galilee, amid

> "Those holy fields,
> Over whose acres walked those blessed feet
> Which eighteen hundred years ago were nailed
> For our advantage to the bitter cross."

CHAPTER XXII.

WITH THE FLOCK.

" Rejoice with them that do rejoice, and weep with them that
weep."—ROMANS xii. 15.

" I must go forth into the town,
To visit beds of pain and death,
Of restless limbs, and quivering breath,
And sorrowing hearts, and patient eyes
That see, through tears, the sun go down,
But nevermore shall see it rise.
The poor in body and estate,
The sick and the disconsolate,
Must not on man's convenience wait."
LONGFELLOW—*Golden Legend.*

LAWRENCE went right among the people—sympathizing with their sorrows, rejoicing in their
simple joys; sitting with the harvesters as they
partook of their frugal meal beneath the beech trees'
shade; walking with the ploughman as he turned
the furrows in the field; talking with the blacksmith
at his forge; sitting with the shoemaker in his little
stall; snatching a word with the stable-boy at the
inn; taking some fish, caught with his own hands,
to old Widow Beddoes; and reading the Bible and
Wesley's hymns to old blind Father Maynard.

One of his most difficult tasks was answering the

catechism of questions which Father Hawkins' shrewd, intelligent wife Peggy asked him every week concerning what was going on all over the world. An alert, brisk old body she was, with a cheek like a peach, an eye like a sloe, a frame that seemed made of steel springs that never got tired and never wore out, and a tongue—but here all comparison fails us. And her mind was as active as her body. The *Christian Guardian* made its weekly visit to their cabin, for, though Father Hawkins could not read, his wife could, and that to better purpose than many who read more. Like a window opened out of a prison into the great, busy, bustling world was the weekly visit of that speculum of the world's and Church's progress—the much-prized household friend.

Could weary, hard-worked editors but know the joy, the deep delight, the food for the insatiable craving for knowledge felt by many who have no other means of gratifying it than the weekly paper, that they have the happiness to impart, they would feel a compensation for all the sweat of brain that they have undergone.

There were no churches as yet on the Centreville mission. The preaching was in school-houses, barns, or the shanties of the settlers. The congregations came from near and far, mostly on foot, a few on horseback, and sometimes a family in a lumber waggon—no other vehicle could stand the rocks and corduroy roads. The school-house at Centreville was always crowded—one would wonder where all the people came from. The women, in all sorts of toilets, frequently with straw hats or poke bonnets, sat on one side. The men, often in their shirt sleeves, on the other. The hard, backless seats were a prophylactic against sleep, and happy was he who got one next the wall where he could support his weary spine. The young men and boys hung around the door, discussing the points of the few horses that drove up, and clustering around outside the open windows as the singing began.

It was an excellent school in which to learn extempore preaching. There was no desk to support notes or manuscript, and unless the speaker could keep the attention of his audience, those about the windows would stroll off to the woods, and sometimes even those inside of the door.

The preacher was also obliged to learn self-possession. He must not be put out by trifles. A commotion among the horses that took half of the men outside, or a little disagreement among the dogs under the seats that could not be settled till both belligerents were kicked out, must not disturb him. Nor must the presence of a dozen children, more or less, some of them of a very tender age. Two or three wandering about the floor, occasionally climbing on the preacher's platform, and as many crying at once, must not throw him off his mental balance. In this school many a Methodist preacher has learned the art of sacred oratory. It is better than putting pebbles in one's mouth and haranguing the ocean waves after the Demosthenic example.

The singing was an important feature at these services. At Centreville, Brother Orton, a tall man with a large nose, a small mouth, a weak, irresolute chin, and glassy eyes, but with a sweet and powerful voice, led the singing. He was assisted by Squire Hill, a man of intensely florid complexion—indeed, of almost a brick-dust colour—with a black tie wound around his neck almost to the point of strangulation, who pitched the tunes on a high-keyed flute, which he carried in a green baize bag. As he manipulated this instrument, which seemed to require an immense quantity of wind, the good brother seemed at times in danger of apoplexy, so red in the face did he become.

Yet there was nothing grotesque or indecorous in these services. Indeed, the spectacle was one of great moral sublimity. Here were a number of toil-worn men and women, bowed down by daily labour and worldly care, wresting a living with much difficulty from a rugged, if in parts a fertile, soil. But for these elevating, ennobling, spiritual services, which lifted their thoughts above the things of earth and time, and set them on things in heaven and eternal, they would sink into utter materialism, almost like the oxen that they drove. But now, through these religious influences, they were raised to the dignity of men, and, in many cases, to the fellowship of saints. Such has been, and such is still, the mission of Methodism in many parts of our country.

The week-night preachings, at "early candle-light," in schools or private houses, were much less formal than the Sunday services. Men and women came in their working clothes, the former sometimes barefoot, the latter with a shawl over their heads. Several brought lanterns or pine knots by which to find their way home through the woods. Others brought candles inserted in the half of a potato or turnip or in the neck of a bottle—the latter kind of candlestick was so precious as to be rather rare.

Full of pathos were the humble rustic funerals, which always called forth the deepest sympathy of that simple rural community. One took place not long after Lawrence arrived. It was that of a poor widow, the mother of a number of young children. Her great concern in her last hours was for them, and she prayed God with great earnestness to be a Father to her fatherless and motherless babes. Lawrence begged her to lay aside her apprehensions, and although not knowing how it would be accomplished, yet full of faith that some way would be found, he promised her that he would see them cared for. With that promise, as a pillow under her dying head, and the hope of meeting them in a better world in her heart, the loving mother seemed to die content.

The neighbours, poor as they were, were very kind. Father Hawkins, rich in faith, if poor in this world's goods, took two of the children.

"Peggy an' Oi be lonesome by times when us thinks of oor oan pretty bairns buried long years sin' in the green churchyard o' Chumleigh, in dear old Devon. They'll be like gran'childer to us in oor old age in this strange land. An' the good Lord, that never forsook us yet, 'll send us food;" and the old man wiped a tear from his eyes, as if longing for the better country, even the heavenly.

"Our house is purty full o' childer," said cheery Hophni Perkins, "like a press bustin' out with noo wine, as the Scriptur' says; but I guess we can take one o' these poor little motherless creeturs. Can't us, mother?"

"Course we can," said his wife Jerusha, her great motherly heart already enfolding the little orphan in its wealth of love.

"Motherliest woman that I ever see," said Hophni proudly. "She nusses all the sick lambs, an' raises chickens that ther own mother gives up. Even the calves an' pigs thrives better under her than anybody else. Powerful smart woman she is."

So the poor children all found homes among these humble but brave-souled people. Even the baby was adopted by a young mother who had just lost her own "pretty little Izrel;" and, "Who knows but the Lord has sent me this in his stead?" she devoutly said.

On the day of the funeral, although it was the height of the wheat harvest, the whole neighbourhood assembled from near and far to pay their last sad tribute of respect to the mother of the children thus adopted. After reading the Scriptures and prayer amid the solemn hush that always falls upon a house in which lies the unburied dead, the plain black-stained coffin, amid the sobs of the children, was carried to a rough waggon and borne to the school-house, which was near the little "God's Acre" already set apart as the seed-plot of the sowing for the harvest of the resurrection morn.

In the seats near the desk sat the motherless children, the younger ones with a look of wondering curiosity on their faces, and other relatives of the deceased. It was touching to notice their attempts to provide symbols of bereavement—the faded and threadbare mourning dress, the meagre black ribbon, and the little wisps of crape.

In the solemn presence of the dead, Lawrence faithfully addressed the living on the momentous lesson of the occasion—a lesson which, in this simple community, had not lost its force through frequency and familiarity. As he prayed for the bereaved ones at the close of his sermon and for the orphaned children, hearty amens went up from many lips, and, we doubt not, from every heart.

The relatives of the departed then approached the open coffin to take their last long lingering farewell of the beloved form that they should see no more. Serene and peaceful was now that toil-worn face with the holy calm which comes when God giveth His beloved sleep—a beam of sunlight, glinting through the window, lighting it up as with the halo of a saint. The thin and wasted hands that had ceased from their labour for ever, were folded on the pulseless breast, and held in their cold death-clasp a cluster of ripe wheat ears and blue-eyed flax flowers—symbols of the resurrection unto everlasting life.

" All was ended now, the hope and the fear and the sorrow,
   All the aching of heart, the restless, unsatisfied longing."

Life's weary wheels at last stood still.

As the children's kisses fell on the pale cold lips of the unanswering clay, their heartrending sobs filled the room, and many a mother wept in sympathy, and even hoary-headed men furtively wiped the tears from

their eyes.   Lawrence, though accustomed to restrain
his feelings, fairly broke down, and sobbed his sorrow
with those motherless children.

Little Mary, three years old, uncomprehending the
awful mystery of death, broke the silence with the
artless question, " Why don't mother wake up ?   She
always did when I touched her face.   Won't she wake
any more ? "

And the baby, in the arms of its new mother,
laughed and crowed, as unconscious of its loss as the
humming-birds, flitting like winged jewels in the sunlight without.

Slowly, tenderly, reverently, devout men bore the
dead to her burial, lifting the coffin as softly as if
they feared to awake the sleeper within.   As they
walked to the little graveyard, not far off, the rustic
congregation followed, reverently singing those words
of holy consolation :

> " Hear what the voice from heaven proclaims
> For all the pious dead !
> Sweet is the savour of their names,
> And soft their dying bed.'

As Lawrence for the first time read the sublime
burial service of our Church, hallowed by the pious
associations of centuries * of use in crowded church-
yards in the dear old motherland, or by the lonely
graves of the English-speaking race throughout the
world, a solemn awe came over his soul.   At the
words, " earth to earth, dust to dust, ashes to ashes,"
as the clods fell with hollow sound on the coffin lid,
they seemed like a warning knell to many a heart,
and by more than one soul, by the side of that open
grave, was the solemn vow recorded to serve God in
newness of life—to walk as in the shadow of eternity
and on the very verge of the other world.

As the grave was filled up and gently and smoothly
sodded over with many a tender pat of the spade, as

* It is substantially that of King Edward VI.'s Prayer Book.

if to shelter the sleeper from the approaching winter
storms, even little Mary seemed to realize the utter-
ness of the parting, and wept bitterly for her " dear
mamma, covered up in the cold dark ground."

But the birds sang on, and the flowers bloomed
still, and the lengthening shadows crept across the
ripened wheat fields, and the great world whirled on
as it will still when all of us are folded in its bosom
for ever.

CHAPTER XXIII

A BACKWOODS OASIS.

"Wide was his parish, and houses fer asonder,
But he ne left nought for no rain ne thonder,
In sicknesse and in mischief to visite
The ferrest in his parish, moche and lite
Upon his fete, and in his hand a staf."
CHAUCER—*Canterbury Tales.*

ONE of Lawrence's week-night appointments was some twenty miles up the shores of the lovely Lakes Muskoka and Rosseau. During the summer he went in Father Hawkins's boat, and greatly enjoyed the trip. The pure air, bright sky, and swift motion of the boat, bounding over the waves before a brisk breeze, seemed to exhilarate like wine. The picturesque scenery, bold rocky shores, cool-grey lichen-covered crags, and innumerable islets of every size and shape and of surpassing loveliness, gratified his fine taste for beauty of landscape. His welcome from the simple settlers was of the warmest character, although his accommodation was often of the scantiest.

Almost everywhere a log schoolhouse was available for worship ; for in this favoured land of ours the schoolmaster and the missionary are the twin pioneers of civilization, and the remotest hamlets have their temple of learning, which is also frequently the temple

A PICTURESQUE BIT IN
MUSKOKA.

OLD-TIME CANADIAN GRIST MILL.

of God. The veteran hero of the conflicts of early Methodism in Canada for the equal rights and privileges which it now enjoys, by giving his ripest years to the upbuilding of a comprehensive common school system, has erected for himself a monument more lasting than brass, and has conferred upon his country a boon more precious than gold. In this remote region the strong pulsations of the vigorous personal influence of Dr. Ryerson—a name never to be mentioned in Canada without loving reverence—made itself strongly felt in diffusing the elements of that intellectual and moral education which alone can make a nation wise and strong and great.

Lawrence visited the school on the first day of his visit to Owen's Corners, as the neighbourhood was called, and was warmly greeted by the teacher, an exceedingly intelligent gentleman. On the walls were maps and charts, and all the essential apparatus for conquering that glorious kingdom of knowledge, which, like the kingdom of heaven, is entered only by becoming as a little child.* The key of all knowledge was placed in each of those little hands. On the seats were a number of bright-eyed, bare-footed boys and girls, as quick-witted as any that will be found in our most favoured cities. Lawrence, at the invitation of the teacher, talked for a few minutes to the "village Hampdens" and, as yet, "mute, inglorious Miltons" of the school, in a way that made their eyes flash and sparkle.

"Now, boys," he said, "I want you to play with all your might when you are at it." Cunning fellow! he knew the way to a boy's heart. He had their ears at once, and they thought him an exceedingly orthodox preacher.

"But," he went on, infixing the barbed truth he had so deftly winged, " when you study, I want you to

---

* This expression, or one something like it, occurs somewhere in Lord Bacon's writings ; we think in his *Instauratio Scientiarum.*

study with all your might, too ; as if you would bore
a hole through the book with your eyes, you know."
With this intense figure a lesson was burnt in, as it
were, into the minds of these boys—a lesson of in-
comparable importance for winning the victory in the
battle of life.

Mr. Norris, the teacher, insisted on making Lawrence
his guest. His abode was humble, but bore evidence
of refinement. Flowers without and within, snowy
curtains, spirited pencil and crayon sketches on the
wall, and the thousand nameless indications of female
taste—felt rather than seen—made the little cottage
seem to Lawrence like an oasis in the wilderness.

"Blessed is he that cometh in the name of the
Lord," said the schoolmaster's kind, motherly wife,
when Lawrence was introduced. His daughter, tall,
graceful, with soft brown eyes and a wealth of
clustering curls, received the stranger with a dignified
courtesy that, thought Lawrence, would have become
a duchess. Books, comprising the best English-
classics and poetry, a volume of Corneille and Dante
in the original, music, a cabinet organ, and drawing
materials, indicated the cultivated tastes of the inmates
of that backwoods shanty, as it might almost be
called.

"You must make this your home," said Mrs. Norris,
"whenever you are at Owen's Corners," an invitation
which Lawrence very gladly accepted.

"I feel as if you belonged to us," said her hospitable
husband. Was it an unconscious prophecy? "My
father was a Wesleyan minister in England, and I
was an old Woodhouse Grove boy, so that I almost
belong to the fraternity myself."

Very pleasant was the evening talk about Dr. Dixon,
Dr. Bunting, Dr. Beaumont, and other great lights of
the English pulpit ; of Samuel Budgett, that merchant
prince of Methodism, in whose great establishment
Mr. Norris had been a confidential clerk ; and of

boyish pranks and schoolday adventures at Woodhouse Grove. Pleasant was the converse with the
hostess about the lovely scenery of the winding Avon
and the Mendip Hills; of the courtly society of those
ancient cities, Bath and Wells; of the strange, sad
story of Chatterton, "the marvellous boy;" and of
the forged poems, "wroten by the gode prieste Thomas
Rowley, of Bristowe." But more pleasant still was
the time spent over the cabinet organ with the fair
Edith, and in sympathetic converse on music and the
recent poetry of Tennyson and Longfellow, which lay
upon the table.

This refined family, apparently buried in the woods,
seemed yet content. The father was able to procure
farms for his boys—an Englishman's ambition, but
scarcely possible to gratify in the crowded old country;
and he could bring up and educate his large family more
cheaply in Canada than at "home," as he still called
the dear old land. He was fond of shooting and fishing,
and here he had it of the finest at his door. Home is
woman's kingdom, and the house-mother found ample
employment therein. And Edith, assisting her father
in the school, was saved from the *ennui* and aching
vacuity that curses an idle life; and developed and
strengthened both intellectual and moral character by
enthusiastic zeal in teaching and in study. The visits
of Lawrence were a mutual pleasure. He was always
cordially welcomed, and it may be surmised that he
did not neglect to visit regularly his appointment at
" The Corners."

One night at the close of the service in the school-
house a sturdy figure strode forward from the shadow,
concealed by which it had been unnoticed, and grasped
Lawrence warmly by both hands, as if it had laid hold
on the handles of a plough.

"But I be dreadful glad to see ye," exclaimed our
old friend Jim Dowler, for it was no other than he, as
he vigorously shook Lawrence's hands. " I knowed it

must be you from the description, though they couldn't
tell your name. I'd 'a' walked fifty miles to hear ye."

"However did you get here?" asked Lawrence,
warmly returning his greeting.

"Didn't ye know that I'd tuk up land on the Seguin?
Two hunnerd acres, half of it on the intervale by the
river, as good land as ever ye see, an' the rest will
make capital stun pastur. An' I've got a house an'
wife, an' two cows an' a hoss—rid him over to see ye
—it's only 'bout a dozen miles north of this—blazed
path most o' the way—an' I've got jest the cheekiest
young un ye ever did see; " and with each clause of the
enumeration he gave Lawrence a poke in the ribs of a
very emphatic character, as he fairly chuckled, like a
schoolboy, with delight. "An' I owes it all to you,
as I may say."

"How is that?" asked Lawrence.

"Why, I owe to you an' Methodism all I am an' all
I've got. Ef you hadn't tuk hold o' me, I'd 'a' been
a poor drunken sot hangin' round Slocum's tavern.
An' now, bless the Lord, I'm happy as the day is long."
And he looked like it, his ruddy countenance beaming
with joy.

"You must come an' see me," he said, "an' give us
a preach. They's some Millerites got in thar, an' they
kind o' stumbles some folks as ain't got the root o'
the matter in 'em. They don't stumble me, hows'ever,
though I don't understand all 'bout the number o' the
beast, an' the seven heads, an' ten horns, an' all the
rest o' it. *I* don't b'lieve, fer my part, that the world's
a-goin' to everlastin' smash, jes' as things is a-gettin'
fairly into gear an' good runnin' order. It's gettin'
better every day, *I* b'lieve," said this happy optimist
philosopher. "Leastways," he devoutly added, "it's
better for me, I know, than afore I know'd you, an' it
may be better for every one if they likes."

Shortly after, Lawrence started to visit Dowler's
Neighbourhood, as it was called. He took a bark

canoe, with which, in this land of lakes and streams,
one can go almost anywhere, and, after paddling
through a couple of lakes and crossing as many portages with his light canoe, not more than thirty pounds'
weight, on his back, he struck the head-waters of the
Seguin. Down the swift current and arrowy rapids of
that river he glided, and soon came to a small clearing
and log-house. Warmer welcome man never had than
he received from his kind host.

"Mary, here's Brother Temple, as ye've often hearn
me tell on—my spiritooal father, God bless 'im. Yes,
Sir, this is my Mary, as I tell'd ye about ; ain't she
jes' as handsome as a pictur, now? An' what d'ye
think o' that fer a boy ?" rattled on the happy man,
as he snatched a chubby baby, like one of Perugino's
rosy cherubs, from his cradle—a sap trough on rockers,
with a pillow in it—and tossed it as high as the rafters
of the ceiling.

"We call 'im Lawrence, ye know fer who ; an' who
knows but the Lord 'll make a preacher of 'im yet?
He's got voice enough when he cries, hasn't he,
mother?" he said, addressing the blushing young
matron, who laughed assent.

While the hired boy was sent to summon the neighbours far and near to preaching, "at early candlelight,"
Lawrence walked over the farm with his host, and
admired the growing crops in the tiny clearing.

"Are you not rather far from market here?" he
asked very naturally. "What do you do with your
crops ?"

"What do we do with 'em? Why, we eat 'em, of
course. Got market near enough for that, I 'low. I
takes the wheat down in a scow to Beattie's Mill,
down the river 'bout eighteen miles, and gets it ground,
an' dickers some at the store for tea an' sugar an' boots
an' stuff for clothes. Dreffle smart fellows them
Beatties is. They runs the hull consarn at the Sound
—Parry Sound, ye know—theirselves jes' about. An'

they won't 'low no liquor sold in the village, neither
Boun' to be a big place, that. Thar wuz a great camp-
meetin' down thar, too, an' hunnerds of Injuns—the
purtiest place ye ever see—a reg'lar wall o' rock all
around, a'most like the mountains round about Jerusalem, ye know."

" You never heard anything of O'Neal or Evans, or
any of the lumbermen, I suppose?" asked Lawrence,
as they talked of old times and camp life.

" Didn't I, though?" replied Jim. " I wuz into
Beattie's store when I wuz down the river with a grist
last week, when who should I see thar a-buyin' a sou'-
wester an' an oil-cloth pea-jacket, but Dennis O'Neal!

" ' Is it meself I am, or am I dramin'?' says he.

" ' This is me, anyhow,' says I, an' with that he shuk
me fist as if he'd got hold o' the boat's tiller. An' I
walked down to see his vessel—the *Betsy Jane*—
loadin' at Beattie's mill for Oswego, an' he showed me
his Bible, an' he tell'd me he had a Bible-class in the
fo'cas'l' every Sunday."

" That's good news," said Lawrence; " I wish I could
know how Evans got on."

" Small joy ther'd be in that," said Dowler with a
sigh. " Dennis, he tell'd me all about it, an' a sad
story it is. Soon as he got his wages at Quebec, he
got on the biggest kind o' spree, an' drinked an'
drinked, as if to make up for the time he'd lost in the
camp, when he couldn't get none. An' Dennis, he
tried to look after him, but when he wuz drunk
he wuz awful 'busive—larned to box at Oxford, ye
know—don't think he larned much else, tho'—an'
the crimps and land-sharks got him into one of the
low taverns on Champlain Street and robbed him, and
then they wuz a-shippin' him as a hand on a vessel
bound fer Jamaicy, an' he wuz so drunk that he slipped
between the wharf an' the boat; an' the tide wuz
runnin' fast, an' he got drownded afore they could get
hold of him.

" Next day the river p'lice got his body on the ebb tide, and the crowner found his right name sewed inside his vest.—Fitz de somethin'—a mighty aristocratic name—an' the port chaplain writ to his folks at some Park or other in Sussex, an' he wuz burried in the strangers' graveyard at the cost o' the city—him that wuz a lord's son an' had the chance o' sich good eddication at that old Brasenose he talked on."

Lawrence felt profoundly sad over the tragic ending of this misspent life. He could not help contrasting its utter shipwreck of all its advantages with the manly usefulness of the humbly born and utterly neglected Jim Dowler. The latter, he learned, in the absence of the circuit preacher at " Dowler's Appointment," sometimes read one of Wesley's sermons, with comments of his own, the rude vernacular and shrewd sense of which blended without any suggestion of incongruity in the minds of his hearers with the plain and nervous English of the learned Fellow of Oxford. Thus does Methodism, with marvellous adaptation, employ the humblest as well as the highest abilities for the glory of God and the salvation of souls.

CHAPTER XXIV.

"T is noble ensample to his shepe he yaf,
That first he wrought and afterwards he taught.
Out of the Gospel he the wordes caught."
CHAUCER—*Canterbury Tales.*

AS Lawrence sailed homeward on the lake in the soft light of a September day, he became aware of a pungent odour in the air, and soon after of a dense smoke drifting from the land. He thought nothing of it, however, but next morning Mr. Perkins remarked :

"The fire's a-gettin' nearer; I wish the wind 'ud change—been burnin' in the woods north there better'n a week."

All day the smoke grew denser, darkening the sun and irritating the eyes. During the night the flames could be seen leaping from tree to tree in the forest that engirdled the little clearing, and running rapidly along the ground in the dry brushwood. The tall pines could be seen burning like gigantic torches in the darkness, and then toppling over with a crash, scattering the sparks in a brilliant shower far and wide, to extend the work of destruction. Great

A BACKWOODS SAW MILL.

A STILL SEQUESTERED NOOK.

tongues of flame hissed and crackled like fiery serpents enfolding their prey.

No human effort could avail aught to withstand or
avert this fiery plague. Only the good providence of
God, by sending rain or turning the wind, could stay
its progress. The next day was intensely hot. The
earth seemed as iron and the heavens as brass.

> " All in a hot and copper sky
> The bloody sun at noon
> Right up above the *trees* did stand,
> No bigger than the moon."

It seemed like the terrors that followed the trumpet
of the fifth angel in the Apocalypse : " There arose
a smoke out of the pit like the smoke of a great
furnace ; and the sun and the air were darkened by
reason of the smoke of the pit."

On came the flames, roaring like a hurricane. The
heat became unendurable, the smoke almost stifling.
The cattle fled to the streams and stood in the deepest
pools, sniffing the heated air. The water became
gradually warm as it flowed over the heated rock and
through the burning woods ; and the fish that were in
it floated on the surface in a dead or dying state.
Fences were torn down, and broad spaces of earth
were turned up by the plough, to break the progress
of the deluge of fire—before which stacks of hay and
straw were licked up like tinder.

Many of the villagers stored their little valuables,
and as much of their grain as they could, in the under-
ground roothouses, and banked them up with earth.
Many had abandoned everything and fled to the is-
lands. Lawrence, with most of the men, remained to
fight the flames till the last moment. When compelled to fly, they sought the shore, where they had
moored a boat as a means of escape at the last
moment. But, O horror ! the lapping of the waves
and the fierce wind created by the fire had loosened

the boat, but insecurely fastened, and it was rapidly drifting away. All hope of escape seemed cut off—the men were about to plunge into the water, as preferring death by drowning to death by fire.

"Let us die like brave men, if die we must," said Lawrence, "trusting in God. He will be with us as He was with His servants in the fiery furnace."

"Father," cried Tom Perkins, a boy of thirteen, "I know a cave where we can hide."

"Quick, my son, show us the way," was the eager reply.

"This way, up the stream a bit—near that cedar root. The bears used to live in it ;" and he pointed out a concealed entrance, through which they crawled into a small grotto, caused by a dislocation of the strata.

"God hath opened for us a cleft in the rock. He will keep us as in the hollow of His hand," said Lawrence, with a feeling of religious exaltation he had never felt in moments of safety.

On came the flames, roaring louder and louder. The crackling of faggots and falling of trees were like the rattle of musketry and firing of cannon in a battle. The smoke and heat penetrated the grotto. They were almost perishing with thirst.

"I hear the trickling of water," said Lawrence. "I will try to find it. Lie low on your faces so as not to inhale the smoke. Here is the water," he cried, as he found it ; "now wet your handkerchiefs and tie them over your heads," he said, as he did the same himself ; and they all found the greatest relief therefrom.

At last the fiery wave seemed to have passed away. They crawled from their refuge to view the desolation the fire had wrought. The ground was still hot and smoking, many of the trees were still burning, and everything was scathed and scarred and blackened with the flames. Perkins's house was burned, but his **barn**, which he prized more, was, with its contents, spared—saved by the adjacent clearing and fallow.

By a special providence, as it seemed to these simple-minded men, unversed in the sceptical objections to the efficacy of prayer, the wind had veered so as to blow the flames away from the village. This they devoutly attributed to their prayers in the cave. That night a copious rain fell, and further danger was averted.

Mr. Perkins's neighbours made a "bee" to help him to rebuild his house, and turned out in full force on that important occasion. Lawrence, a fine athletic specimen of muscular Christianity, turned to with a will, and swung his axe and rolled his logs with the best of them, as "to the manner born." He won thereby the profound respect of several of the young men, who were more impressed with his prowess with the axe than by his eloquence in the pulpit.

Soon a larger and better house than the one destroyed was erected, so that Hophni said "the fire wuz a sort o' blessin' in disguise." He "feared he wuz a-takin' better keer o' his crops and beasts than of his wife and chil'en ; so the Lord jes' gin 'im a hint to make them kind o' comfortable, too."

Lawrence was very anxious to have a church built at Centreville, the head of the circuit, for the purpose of holding quarterly meetings and the like, as well as to accommodate the growing congregation. Some of the wise men of the village gravely shook their heads, and said it was impossible after the fire. But the zealous young preacher was determined to try. He therefore went round with his subscription book for contributious. These were mostly in "kind" or in labour.

Squire Hill gave a lot in the village, which did not count for much, as land was plenty, and real estate, even on the front street of Centreville, was not worth much more than that three miles distant. But he

11

promised, moreover, all the nails, glass, and putty required, which counted for a great deal, as these articles were not in such plenty as land in Muskoka.

Hophni Perkins gave all the pine wanted for the frame, as a "thank offerin'" to the Lord for sparing his barn and crops, and a liberal subscription besides. His brother Phinehas, who owned a sawmill on the creek, gave all the sawn lumber required.

Father Hawkins could not give anything else, so he promised to make the shingles during the winter. The village painter promised to do the painting if the materials were provided, which was soon done by subscription.

A grand "bee" was accordingly made to get out the material. Axemen felled the tallest, straightest trees for sills, frame, plates, joists, rafters, purlines, and all the appurtenances thereof.

"It reminds me," said Father Hawkins, "of Hiram and his workmen getting out the timbers for the house of God at Jerusalem." Teams of oxen and horses dragged them to the site of the building. Others drew stone for the foundation, sand for the plaster, and boards to enclose the building.

Lawrence was the moving spirit of all these activities —the wheel within the wheel—the mainspring of the whole. He it was who drew the plan, got out the estimates, made all the calculations, and was a whole building committee in himself. Nor was he content with directing. He worked with the strongest and most diligent. He mortised sills and plates, and tenoned studs and beams; and another great "bee" was made for putting together and raising the frame.

It was like magic. In the morning the ground was strewn with beams and timbers—the *disjecta membra* of a house. In the evening they were all in their places, and the complete skeleton of the building stood erect in its gaunt proportions, the admiration of not only the village but the entire country-side. Almost, thought Lawrence, might be applied the words of Milton, descriptive of a structure of far other character:

> "Anon out of the earth a fabric huge
> Rose like an exhalation."

But this was only the bony framework. It had yet to be indued with the flesh and skin, so to speak. Everybody who was skilled in carpentry—and in the bush almost everybody learns to be so skilled—gave one, two, or more weeks' work, an'l before winter the church was covered in, and by spring it was nearly finished. Although not of very elaborate architecture, it was an object of great complacency to the entire community, and especially to those who had wrought upon it. Among these were several who had never previously shown any interest in Church matters, but who now became quite zealous in its secular concerns. They soon became more interested, also, in its religious worship, and were brought at last more immediately under the influence of the Gospel. Get a man to give or work for any object, and you have quickened his interest in that object for ever.

CHAPTER XXV.

PERIL AND RESCUE—THE GUIDING STAR.

"It comes—the beautiful, the free,
  The crown of all humanity—
    In silence and alone
    To seek the elected one."
                    LONGFELLOW —*Endymion*.

"A being breathing thoughtful breath,
  A traveller between life and death ;
  The reason firm, the temperate will.
  Endurance, foresight, strength, and skill ;
  A perfect woman, nobly planned,
  To warn, to comfort, and command ;
  And yet a spirit still, and bright
  With something of an angel light."
                              WORDSWORTH.

LAWRENCE did not neglect during the winter to keep up the round of his appointments, far and near, especially, as may be supposed, that at Owen's Corners. On snow-shoes, or on horse-back, or in a rude jumper, how bad soever the weather or the road, he was always at his post. On one occasion when the drifts were so deep that his horse fell down, unable to proceed, he unhitched the out-done animal, left his "jumper". in the snow, and led his horse to the school-house, where a large company were awaiting patiently his confidently expected appearance.

When possible, the frozen lake was chosen as offering a smooth and level road. One night—it was towards spring, and a thaw and rain had weakened the ice—he was overtaken by night some distance from the landing. As it became dark, he hugged the shore pretty closely in order to avoid getting lost on the ice. At length he saw gleaming in the distance a well-known light. It was that of the room in which the fair Edith Norris sat and read and sewed or sketched. Had he been sufficiently familiar with Shakespeare, he would probably have said with Romeo—

> " Yonder's the East, and Juliet is my sun ; "

but he simply thought, " Is that fair creature to be the loadstar of my life ? "

These pleasant reflections, however, were soon ended. Suddenly, in a moment, his horse disappeared, as utterly as if he had been annihilated. Lawrence sprang instantly from the back of his " jumper," but was immersed in the water up to his waist. He managed to scramble out on to the ice, however, and crept carefully around to the head of his horse, which was struggling in the water. He tried, after the backwoods fashion, to bring the animal to the surface by twisting the " lines " around his neck and then to drag him on to the ice. But the ice kept breaking around the edge as often as he attempted this feat.

After struggling alone in the dark with the drowning horse for some time, he resolved to seek help at the landing, more than a mile off. He first drew the points of the shafts well up on the ice, so as to support the animal, and then started for the shore. But he had now completely lost his bearings, and he could not form the least idea where the landing was. He eagerly scanned the horizon, but could only see, looming through the darkness, the shadowy outline of the shore. At length, O joy ! there, far to the left,

gleamed the solitary light which had previously glad-
dened his vision. It became his loadstar in peril
sooner than he had thought. Would its fair mistress
also? He hurried, with sturdy strides, to the shore,
the chill wind piercing his wet clothing. Reaching
the landing, he entered the village tavern, the nearest
house, and cried, "My horse is in the lake. I'll give
ten dollars if you'll get him out."

Four or five sturdy fellows immediately set out
with ropes and a lantern. They spread out in skir-
mishing order over the lake, so as to sweep as much
of its surface as possible. The rising wind blew out
the lantern, and much time was lost in relighting it.

"This way," shouted Lawrence, who had run ahead.
The poor animal, struggling hard in the ice-cold water,
heard his voice, and faintly whinnied a reply. Lawrence
hurried on, and supported the faithful creature's head
till the men came up, when by main force they dragged
him out on the ice. The benumbed animal was able
to walk to the shore, apparently not much the worse
for his icy immersion.

"Gentlemen, you have my warmest thanks," said
Lawrence, when they were reassembled in the bar-
room, and he took out his meagre wallet to divide
among them the promised reward.

"D'ye think we want your money?—not if I know
myself and these jolly fellows," said the landlord, a
burly, good-hearted man, though engaged in a very
nefarious calling. But oftentimes, alas!

> "Evil is wrought by want of thought
>   As well as want of heart."

"Of course we don't," "Not a cent," "D'ye think
we'd resk we're lives for money?" chorused the
entire group.

One pitiful-looking sot, however, who had boozed
by the fire while the others were on the ice, hiccupped
out, "Ye moight treat us to summat, noo ye've getten
yer 'orse as were as good as droonded."

" Gentlemen," said Lawrence, " it is contrary to my principles to treat or be treated to liquor. But I will be obliged, Mr. Landlord, if you will prepare for those gallant men the best coffee supper you can get up."

" Hurrah for the preacher ! " " He's a brick ! " echoed the group, the latter expression being the very quintessence of a backwoods compliment.

Lawrence had been wet for over an hour, and was shivering with the cold. He forewent his purpose of going to the Norris's hospitable house in his then plight, and asked for a bed at the tavern, at the same time ordering a quart of spirits to be taken up to his room, that he might bathe his benumbed limbs.

" It's good sometimes externally, gentlemen," he said, " and that is the only way it is good."

" 'E wants to taak a soop on the sly," said the dis- appointed toper.

" Landlord," said Lawrence, not deigning to notice the insult, " haven't you some strychnine that you use for killing foxes ? "

" Yes. What do you want with it ? " he replied, as he brought a small package from the clock case, in which, for safety, it was hidden.

" Only this," answered Lawrence, as he poured it all into the vessel containing the spirits. " Now, gentle- men," he went on, " I'm not likely to take any of it ' on the sly,' nor any other way. But its poison is no more deadly now than it was before, only a little quicker in its operation, that is all ; " and he bade them a courteous good-night.

" He's a trump," said the landlord, " anyway, for all his notions. Pity he's a preacher. What a politician he'd make with that manner of his'n ! He's nobody's fool, nuther—'cute as a weasel, he is. If he was only runnin' for parliament now, he'd scoop up the votes at the Corners wholesale."

So great was that worthy's admiration of his unusual

guest that he refused next morning to accept anything
for his entertainment over night.

"The men preferred drinks o' whisky all round to
any of yer coffee stuff," he said; "an' I won't ask ye
to pay for what's agin yer principles.   An' as fer
your bed, you're welcome here any time."

Very warm were the congratulations of the Norris
family, who, in consequence of the celerity with which
news travels in the country, even without telegraphs
or telephones, had already heard of his adventure.

As Lawrence told the fair Edith that it was the
light of her lamp that had been the guiding star that
rescued him from the peril in the dark, her eyes were
suffused with a sympathetic emotion. A great hope
dawned like a brighter star in the young man's soul ;
but he strove to put the thought aside as a temptation
that might come between him and the great life-work
to which he was espoused as to a bride—that of
the humble and ill-remunerated toil of a Methodist
preacher.

The winter passed rapidly by. Successful revivals
had taken place at several of the appointments, and
the membership was largely increased. With the
spring thaw the roads broke up, and travel was almost
impossible. To Lawrence's efforts to reach his appointments might almost be applied the words of Milton
descriptive of the progress of a far different character
on a far different mission.

> " O'er bog, or steep, through strait, rough, dense or rare,
> With head, hands, wings or feet pursues his way,
> And swims, or sinks, or wades, or creeps, or flies."

But still he bated not a jot of energy or hopefulness.
As the bright spring weather came—and it comes
with an almost magical transformation in these
northern latitudes—the church was approaching com-
pletion.   Lawrence expected   that   that venerable,
highly-honoured and much-beloved friend of missions,

Dr. Enoch Wood, who has probably opened more churches for the worship of God than any other man in Canada, would conduct the dedication service. But that could not take place till after Conference, and so probably he would not even have the pleasure of witnessing the consecration of the building in whose erection he had toiled so earnestly.

There is probably no class of men in the world who more completely solve by their life of labour the Virgilian riddle :

> " Sic vos non vobis nidificatis aves.
> Sic vos non vobis vellera fertis oves.
> Sic vos non vobis mellificatis apes.
> Sic vos non vobis fertis aratra boves."

They labour, and another enters into their labours. Yet none are more zealous for the upbuilding of the cause of God than they, even in a neighbourhood which they expect soon to leave, probably never to see it again. In no Church is the unselfish, wide-hearted, comprehensive connexional spirit more grandly developed. Their sympathies are not circumscribed by any local limits. The progress of God's work at Gaspe or Red River, nay, at Fort Simpson, on the Pacific, or in Japan, causes the same thrill of happy emotion as a revival on the adjoining circuit.

So Lawrence toiled among these people as though he was to live with them all his life. Or rather, he toiled harder, for he felt that whatever he would do among them he must do at once, for he might never have another opportunity. The people were exceedingly anxious for his return, and requested his reappointment. But they could offer him no inducement beyond a hearty welcome, glad co-operation, hard toil and plenty of it, poor fare, and scanty remuneration. But for just such rewards hundreds of brave, great-hearted men are willing to spend and be spent in the most blessed service of the Divine Master.

CHAPTER XXVI.

THE ACCOLADE.

"Christ to the young man said, 'Yet one thing more;
  If thou wouldst perfect be,
Sell all thou hast and give it to the poor,
  And come and follow Me.'

"Within this temple Christ again, unseen,
  Those sacred words hath said,
And His invisible hands to-day have been
  Laid on a young man's head."
        LONGFELLOW—*Ordination Hymn.*

"O blessed Lord! how much I need
Thy light to guide me on my way!
So many hands that, without heed,
Still touch Thy wounds and make them bleed!
So many feet that, day by day,
Still wander from Thy fold astray!
Unless Thou fill me with Thy light,
I cannot lead Thy flock aright;
Nor, without Thy support, can bear
The burden of so great a care,
But am myself a castaway."
        LONGFELLOW—*Golden Legend.*

AS the Conference was to be held not far from
Northville, Lawrence yielded to the combined
inducement of paying a visit to his home and attending
as an interested spectator the meetings of that august

CONFERENCE SUNDAY IN CANADA.

TRIPLE FALL, MUSKOKA.

body, which he regarded as entrusted with the most important interests in the world—and we are not sure that in this he was very greatly mistaken.

The home-greeting was of the warmest. There was much to hear and much to tell, notwithstanding that almost weekly letters were exchanged between mother or sisters and the absent one. Mary was blossoming into lovely womanhood, and proud was Lawrence as she gave him her sisterly greeting among the June roses, herself more blooming-fair than they. The saintly mother looked more saintly still, wan and worn with care and toil, and the streaks of silver were more abundant in her hair. But the same hallowed light was in her eyes, the same calm peace—the peace of God that passeth all understanding—was on her brow.

The period of the visit was a continual holiday. It was a short drive to the Conference town, and every day Lawrence took his mother or sister to the sessions of that body. It soon assumed a more important relation to him than he had anticipated. On his arrival he was informed by the chairman of his district that the Stationing Committee had put him down again for Centreville Mission ; and, furthermore, that in view of the remoteness and isolation of the field and his own success and maturity of character, beyond his years—here Lawrence blushed and bowed—they had resolved to recommend his ordination "for special purposes"—that is, in order that he might administer the sacraments and celebrate marriage.

This was unexpected, almost startling news ; but as he looked into his heart, he found a feeling neither of exultation, nor of shrinking from his increased responsibilities, but of acquiescence with the will of God, whatever it might be. The Conference assented to the somewhat unusual proposal on account of the special circumstances of the case ; and Lawrence was directed to present himself with the class of probationers whose reception was to take place on the Friday even-

ing, and who were to be ordained on the following
Sabbath. He sought solitude as much as possible
during the interval before these solemn services, that
he might commune with his own heart, and afresh
dedicate himself to God.

That important service, to him one of the most
solemn of his life, when he, so young, so retiring, so
almost morbidly shrinking in his disposition, in the
presence of a vast multitude, including some hundreds
of ministers, was to make his confession of faith and
tell the story of his call to the work of the ministry, at
length arrived. At first he had shrunk from the ordeal,
but as the time drew nigh he felt strangely calm and
sustained by the presence and power of God. His
mother and sister, of course, were in the audience, and
their magnetic eyes drew the gaze of his and inspired
him with their sympathy, till he seemed to forget the
presence of all others than they. When called upon,
he spoke as simply as in a quiet class-meeting in
Muskoka, yet with a suppressed emotion that touched
every heart.

He did not wonder, he said, that he was trying to
serve God. He wondered that he was not trying to
serve Him better. As he spoke of his early consecration to God, of the hallowed spell of his mother's
influence on his young life, in moulding his character,
and in leading him to the Saviour, his voice faltered,
and many an eye was suffused with tears. But that
mother's eyes, into whose depths he gazed, lit up
with a starry splendour, seemed to give him control
over his emotions. Then he spoke of the moulding
influence of the Sabbath-school, of the early strivings
of God's Spirit with his soul, of his yielding to His
blessed influence.

As he spoke of his father as the ideal hero of his
boyhood, of his brave example, of the white flower of
his blameless life, of his triumphant death, and of the
promise made to follow in his footsteps as he had been

a follower of the Lord Jesus, many of the ministers present, who had known and loved the man, carried away by the fervency of their feelings, cried out, "Hallelujah!" "God bless the lad!" "May the father's mantle rest upon the son!" "Amen!" "Praise the Lord!"

Then he spoke of the great help he had received from his fathers in the ministry, and especially from the professors of the college, his brief season at which was an unfading memory of gladness and perpetual impulse to the culture of all his powers. But when he spoke of the great joy of gathering in the first harvest of souls in his far-off mission, his voice deepened and his form seemed to dilate as he rejoiced before God with the joy of those who bring their sheaves with them.

When he, with the other probationers, had sat down, he listened with deep emotion and delight to the wise counsels, the fatherly and brotherly utterances of the senior ministers who moved and seconded or supported their reception. The names of some of these had been for years as familiar to his ears as "household words," and he now saw them and heard their voices, and felt that he was welcomed by these veteran warriors, who had borne the brunt of many a conflict with sin and wrong, to the same holy brotherhood to which they belonged—a grander knighthood than the mail-clad chivalry of arms.

But on the Sabbath his emotions were even deeper, as he listened to the solemn charge of the President of the Conference, and was set apart—as a being consecrated to God for ever—by the laying on of hands of the presbytery. Never did he so feel how high was the dignity, how weighty the office to which he was called, how precious the treasure committed to his care, and how grave the responsibility which he bore. He therefore, while he almost trembled beneath the vows which he took, put his whole soul into the words he uttered in answer to the questions of the President, looking up to God for strength to keep these solemn vows.

As he repeated with the others that sublime hymn of the ages, the *Veni, Creator, Spiritus,* he realized in his soul the blessed unction from above of the Anointing Spirit and the impartation of His sevenfold gifts. As he received in his hands the Holy Bible which was to be the charter of his authority to preach the Word of God and to administer the sacraments in the congregation, he fervently kissed the sacred book, and then pressed it to his heart as his guide and counsellor through life, trusting in whose blessed teachings he hoped at last to go home in triumph to the skies. He grasped it in his hand as the sharp two-edged sword of the Spirit which he was to wield as his battle-brand; and he cried in his heart, as did David when he grasped the mighty sword of Goliath, "Give it me; there is none like it."

During the Conference sessions Lawrence took especial delight in sitting in the gallery of the church with his mother or sister, and listening to the debates. From his chairman, who sometimes joined them, he learned the names of most of the ministers, and sometimes sketches of their often remarkable history. They seemed to him like the warriors of a Homeric battle-field; or rather, for that simile degraded their character, they were the plumed heroes of a nobler chivalry than that of the steel-clad warriors of old— the true Christian knighthood,

> "Whose glory was redressing human wrong,
> Who reverenced their conscience as their king,
> Who spake no slander; no, nor listened to it;"

whose trophies were not garments rolled in blood and brazen helms all battle-stained and dinted, but a world redeemed, regenerated, disenthralled by the mighty manumission of the blood of Christ.

At last came the closing hour of the Conference, and its crowning act, the reading of the stations. The scene rose to the dignity of the morally sublime. The galleries were filled with interested spectators. Every minister was in his place. Several of them were, for the first time, to learn their destiny for the year—often involving the sundering of tender ties, a long and tedious journey, and the seeking of a new home among perfect strangers. The President took the chair with unusual gravity of mien. The grand inspiring battle-hymn was sung—

> " Soldiers of Christ, arise,
> And put your armour on."

A hero-soul looked out of each man's eyes. There was no faltering, no flinching. Each one was ready to accept his fate and go forth .

> " Strong in the strength which God supplies
> Through His Eternal Son."

The Secretary read with a clear, distinct voice the decrees of the Book of Fate which he held in his hands. Every eye was fixed on the speaker. Every sound was hushed. The very ticking of the clock smote with unusual emphasis upon the ear. As Lawrence heard his name read out for Centreville Mission, he bowed his head upon the rail before him and lifted up his heart to God; and when he raised it, by the glad light in his eyes it might be seen that his prayer had been answered.

Not a murmur arose, not a protest was heard in all that assembly against the decisions of that day, although they vitally affected these men in their most intimate and personal relations. Has the world ever witnessed a sublimer spectacle ?

Then they sang again, each man making the words the utterance of his own soul :

" Forth in Thy name, O Lord, I go,
    My daily labour to pursue;
  Thee, only Thee, resolved to know
    In all I think, or speak, or do.

" The task Thy wisdom hath assigned,
    O let me cheerfully fulfil !
  In all my works Thy presence find,
    And prove Thy acceptable will.

" For Thee delightfully employ
    Whate'er Thy bounteous grace hath given ;
  And run my course with even joy,
    And closely walk with Thee to heaven."

With this as their sublime marching song and
battle-hymn, they went forth again on their sacred
crusade—the army of the holy cross—against the
embattled legions of the prince of the power of the
air—to know no truce nor respite till the Great
Captain of their salvation should say to each warrior,
" It is enough ; enter into My joy and sit down on
My throne."

The few days that Lawrence spent at home were
days of hallowed enjoyment. But although they were
to him like an oasis to a weary traveller, he was eager
to be at his field of sacred toil. " I am the King's
messenger," he said, when his mother asked him to
stay a little longer, " and the King's business requires
haste."

" Go, my son," replied that nobler than Spartan
mother. " Had I ten sons, I would give them all to
be the messengers of such a King."

The next day, therefore, Lawrence departed, inspired
with fresh zeal and courage, to labour for the glory of
God amid the rocks and lakes and wilds of Muskoka.
Here, for the present, we must leave him. The story
of his trials and his triumphs, of his discouragements
and successes, of his varied adventures on various
fields of labour, " in the wide waste and in the city
full," and the blending of his fortunes, after many

strange and providential vicissitudes, with those of the fair Edith—this story may be hereafter told. For the present we bid " Farewell " to our kind readers, and " Farewell and God-speed " to LAWRENCE TEMPLE. THE KING'S MESSENGER.

Hazell, Watson, and Viney, Printers, London and Aylesbury.

VALERIA, THE MARTYR OF THE CATACOMBS.

A Tale of Early Christian Life in Rome.

BY THE

. REV. W. H. WITHROW, D.D.

Crown 8vo, with Illustrations.   *Price, 70 cents.*

OPINIONS OF THE PRESS.

"The subject is skilfully handled, and the lesson it conveys is noble and encouraging."—*Daily Chronicle.*

"The story is fascinatingly told, and conveys a vast amount of information."—*The Witness.*

"A charming little book, and as useful as it is pleasant."—*Hastings and St. Leonard's News.*

"Well written and correct in its details and setting."—*Sunday School Chronicle.*

"An interesting and instructive historical tale."—*Sheffield Telegraph.*

"A vivid and realistic picture of the times of the persecution of the early Christians under Diocletian."—*Watchman.*

Barbara Heck:
A Story of Canadian Methodism.

BY

W. H. WITHROW, D.D., F.R.S.C.

Cloth, - 75 cents.

Dr. Withrow's graceful pen gives us in this book in the form of a story the adventures of the little band of Methodists who, with others, forsook the older settlements of the United States on the outbreak of the Revolutionary War and laid the foundations of empire in this then northern wilderness.

Few Canadian books have been so cordially welcomed as this inspiring and spirited story from Dr. Withrow's practised pen. Principal Grant, of Queen's University, makes it the subject of a four-page article in the *Methodist Magazine and Review*, in which he says: "Reading it, a window was opened through which I saw glimpses into the early history of our people."

The *Montreal Witness* gives it nearly three columns of space, and says: "We could wish that thousands besides Methodists would read it to kindle and fan the flame of Canadian patriotism, and that all might learn the imperishable power and beauty of Godliness and true religion in humble life."

WILLIAM BRIGGS, Publisher,
Wesley Buildings, Toronto.

MONTREAL: C. W. COATES.   HALIFAX: S. F. HUESTIS.